The
Darcys of
Derbyshire

ABIGAIL REYNOLDS

WHITE SOUP PRESS

THE DARCYS OF PEMBERLEY

www.pemberleyvariations.com
www.austenvariations.com

Part I

Derbyshire, 1812

"Absolutely not, Lizzy!" Mr. Gardiner crossed his arms over his chest, as unyielding as the gritstone escarpment that rose behind him.

"Oh, very well," Elizabeth said. "I still believe it would be perfectly safe. Look at that gentleman atop the highest tor – he seems perfectly at ease, and he would not have climbed there in fashionable clothing if it were a difficult ascent."

As she watched, the tall gentleman in the distance reached into the empty air in front of him. Was he releasing something? The distance was such it was impossible to make out if anything left his hand. He held his arm outstretched for a minute more, then slowly lowered it. After standing there a short while longer, he disappeared behind the rock outcropping.

Mrs. Gardiner spread the blanket for their picnic. "I know you would like to climb it, Lizzy, but we simply cannot let you go up there alone. I do not have the strength for such an effort, and it would be unfair to ask your uncle to do so, given how much he dislikes heights. It is enough of a privilege to see the amazing shapes nature has created from these rocks, and we shall enjoy the view over the valley as we eat."

It would be the height of ungraciousness to criticize her aunt and uncle's decision. After all, they had been generous enough to invite her to join them on this journey to Derbyshire. It was her business to be satisfied with whatever they offered, or at least to *behave* as if she were content, so she helped her aunt to set out the cold meats and pastries they had brought with them. If she looked longingly at the rock pinnacle from time to time, she managed to say nothing further about it, restricting her comments to the striking view of the valley.

A family with two children, perhaps eight and ten, drove up in a wagon and set off noisily on the rocky path to the rock spires. If children and their mother could climb it, surely Elizabeth could as well! She had to bite her tongue to stop herself from asking to go with them. Although the view from the top would no doubt be extraordinary, it was not that which drew her. There was nothing like the invigorating sensation of being high up, the wild freedom that came from seeing the ground far below her. She had been an inveterate tree climber until she grew too old for such hoydenish behavior. All that was left to her now was walking to the summits of the modest hills near Meryton. This opportunity was a rare one, and she could almost taste her desire to climb to the top.

As they were finishing their meal, the rattle of pebbles falling made Elizabeth glance toward the path once more. The tall gentleman, now wearing a hat, picked his way down the last steep stretch. His form seemed familiar to her, which she attributed to her time watching him atop the tor. Dropping her eyes back to the picnic, she wondered what he had released from the summit.

Mrs. Gardiner's brows drew together. "That gentleman is staring at you in a very odd manner, Lizzy. Is he someone you know?"

"I do not think so," Elizabeth said, but she looked up at him again. Her heart plummeted all the way to her toes when she recognized Mr. Darcy. He started, then seemed immoveable from surprise.

At first she could not believe it was him. He had haunted her thoughts ever since their arrival in Lambton, and most especially since her aunt's suggestion that they tour Pemberley. It had seemed too good to be true when the chambermaid had assured her the Darcy family was not at Pemberley for the summer. Apparently it *was* too good to be true, for there he stood. But *why* was he here, at a spot frequented by travelers and families on holiday? If he had not been at Pemberley two days ago, what would bring him out to see a sight he must be familiar with so soon after his arrival?

And if she was shocked to see him, what must *he* think of *her* presence there? Apart from their brief encounter when he handed her his letter and spoke only one sentence, their last meeting had been the nightmarish evening when she had refused his proposal in the strongest terms and accused him falsely. What a fool she had been to believe Wickham's lies! Her face grew hot, and Mr. Darcy's cheeks were overspread with blushes as well.

Feeling as awkward as a twelve year old caught in mischief, Elizabeth scrambled to her feet and bobbed a curtsey. How mortifying it was to encounter him in such a place! He must despise the very thought of her.

Mr. Darcy, recovering himself, advanced toward Elizabeth. "Miss Bennet, this is an unexpected pleasure," he said, in terms of perfect civility, if not perfect composure. "I hope your family is well."

Elizabeth scarcely dared lift her eyes to his face. "They were quite well when I saw them last, I thank you."

"You have been travelling? Have you been in Derbyshire long?" His accent had none of its usual sedateness.

"Only a few days so far, sir." She was astonished at his civility, but every sentence he uttered was increasing her embarrassment.

He glanced around as if distracted, and his gaze lighted on Mr. and Mrs. Gardiner. "Will you do me the honor of introducing me to your friends?"

This was a stroke of civility for which she was quite unprepared; and despite her discomfiture, she could hardly suppress a smile at his now seeking the acquaintance of some of those very people against whom his pride had revolted. He would be surprised when he discovered who they were, since he seemed to take them now for people of fashion.

The introduction, however, was immediately made; and as she named their relationship to herself, she stole a sly look at him, to see how he bore it; and it was not without the expectation of his decamping as fast as he could from such disgraceful companions. That he was *surprised* by the connection was evident; he sustained it however with fortitude, and so far from going away, entered into conversation with Mr. Gardiner. Elizabeth could not but be pleased, could not but triumph. It was consoling to know she had some relations for whom there was no need to blush. She listened most attentively to all that passed between them, and gloried in every expression, every sentence of her uncle, which marked his intelligence, his taste, or his good manners.

She blushed again and again over the perverseness of the meeting. Mr. Darcy's behaviour was so strikingly altered. What could it mean? That he should even speak to her was amazing! But to speak with such civility, to enquire after her family! Never in her life had she seen his manners so little dignified, never had he spoken with such gentleness as on this unexpected meeting. What a contrast it offered to his last address in Rosings Park, when he put his letter into her hand! She knew not what to think, nor how to account for it.

"We are taking great pleasure in the scenic delights of Derbyshire," said Mr. Gardiner, gesturing to the view across the valley. "We have nothing to match this in London."

"Indeed not," said Mr. Darcy. "Do you plan to climb to the top after your repast?"

Mr. and Mrs. Gardiner exchanged a glance. "This is as far as we intend to go," said Mrs. Gardiner. "Neither my husband nor I care for climbing to such heights."

"And you, Miss Bennet?"

Elizabeth clasped her hands so tightly that her fingers ached. "I will remain with my aunt and uncle," she said carefully. "Naturally, they do not wish me to go up alone."

With a puzzled look, Darcy said, "It is a relatively easy ascent, even for a lady, and the view is spectacular. My mother climbed it often. This was a favorite place of hers."

One of his mother's favorite places was atop a rocky tor in the middle of nowhere? Elizabeth had never stopped to consider what Darcy's mother would have been like, but she would have expected her to be fashionable and ladylike, not a climber of rocks.

"I appreciate the reassurance, Mr. Darcy," said Mr. Gardiner amiably. "Still, it is quite a high perch, is it not? I would not want to take any chances with our Lizzy. But would you care to join us for a glass of wine before you depart?"

Darcy hesitated, and then said, "Thank you. That would be most refreshing." He joined them on the blanket, choosing the space between Elizabeth and Mrs. Gardiner, and accepted a glass from Mrs. Gardiner.

Elizabeth could make no sense of it. That he should attempt to be civil was surprising enough, but that he should accept such an informal invitation when it forced him into her company – it was shocking. She could not help but be aware of his nearness when he was only inches away from her.

"Do you come here often, Mr. Darcy?" asked Mr. Gardiner.

"As often as I can. Each summer I try to make a point of visiting."

"You must be very fond of the view, then."

Mr. Darcy hesitated, then glanced at Elizabeth. "This place holds special meaning for my family. Both my parents loved it; and after my mother's death, my father came here to honor her memory. It became a tradition for us to pay a visit each year on the anniversary of her death. Since losing my father, I have continued to do so on my own. I remember her bringing me here when I was a young child, and pointing out how very different familiar places can look from above. On a clear day, it is possible to make out my own home, Pemberley, in the distance."

"Is that so?" asked Mr. Gardiner. "It must be nearly ten miles! We passed by it yesterday and almost stopped for a tour of the park."

"*You* were at Pemberley?" asked Mr. Darcy.

Mortified, Elizabeth said quickly, "My aunt wished to see the grounds there. She remembers them fondly from her younger days when she lived nearby. Unfortunately, she was too tired after our travels to walk so far." Oh, how embarrassing this was! What must he think of her, that she would even *consider* visiting the estate of a man she had refused with such unkindness?

The news did not seem to disturb him, since he turned to Mrs. Gardiner and asked, "You are from Derbyshire?"

"Yes, I was raised in Lambton, where we are presently staying. I visited Pemberley's grounds several times during my youth. I still recall how each turn in the path seemed to take us to a lovelier vista than the one before it."

"I thank you. The current landscape garden is the work of my parents." Darcy turned to Elizabeth almost hesitantly. "If you should have the time during your travels, I would be happy to show you Pemberley."

"We would not wish to impose," said Elizabeth hurriedly. "Before we left Bakewell yesterday morning, we were given to understand you were not immediately expected in the country, or we should not have even considered stopping." And why *was* he back already? Was it solely to perform this memorial for his mother?

"That had been my plan, but business with my steward occasioned me to go ahead of the rest of my party. I arrived home yesterday late in the day, but I assure you your visit would be a pleasure, not an imposition."

Mrs. Gardiner, who was sitting across from Elizabeth, gave her a look expressive of her wonder at this civility. Elizabeth said nothing, but it gratified her exceedingly; the compliment must be all for herself. Her astonishment, however, was extreme; and she could not help wondering why he was so altered. From what had it proceeded? It could not be for *her* sake that his manners were thus softened! Her reproofs at Hunsford could not have worked such a change as this, unless perhaps...surely he could not still care for her?

The Gardiners spoke for a while of their tour of Derbyshire, until Mr. Darcy said, "I do not wish to interpose myself, but if Miss Bennet still desires to climb the tor, I would be happy to accompany her and assure her safety. It is not a long walk, no more than half an hour each way."

Elizabeth's surprise was only exceeded by her longing to accept his offer. It might be uncomfortable to be alone with Mr. Darcy after all that had passed between them, but she would suffer far worse than that for the opportunity to climb the tor. She looked pleadingly at her uncle.

"Well," said Mr. Gardiner slowly, "I suppose there would be no harm in it, since you know the place so well; and you and Lizzy are acquaintances of some standing. Poor Lizzy has been trying so hard not to look disappointed we would not allow her to climb it alone."

"Oh, thank you!" she cried, unsure if she were speaking to her uncle, Mr. Darcy, or both; but she could not disguise her pleasure at the opportunity. "I would enjoy that very much. It is exceedingly kind of you, Mr. Darcy, to take the time when you have only just descended from the tor yourself."

"It is a sight that should not be missed," he said seriously. "My mother would have insisted upon it." He stood and offered Elizabeth his hand.

Accepting his assistance more out of politeness than necessity, she rose to her feet. "Then I am grateful to your mother as well. I confess I was sorely disappointed not to have the opportunity."

His mouth crooked in a slight smile. "So I gathered from the longing glances you kept casting in that direction. It seemed odd such a great walker would not wish to explore further."

Elizabeth did not miss the pointed look shared between her aunt and uncle at this juncture, but she limited herself to promising them she would return soon. She only hoped Mr. Darcy had been oblivious to it. To have him think her family had expectations of him would be mortifying!

Her heart beat quickly as they set off on the path, which was narrow enough to require him to go ahead of her. It was something of a relief since she hardly knew what to say to him. That he should show her kindness after her vituperative refusal of his proposal demonstrated a more forgiving nature than she would have thought him to possess. His remarks about his mother had also surprised her. She had known, of course, that he must have had a mother. After all, everyone did, but she had never before conceived of Darcy's mother as an actual person, one to whom he might have had an attachment. If she had ever given it a thought, she would have imagined her as a perfect lady whose accomplishments tended towards such things as embroidery and watercolors, not as someone who enjoyed the outdoors and loved to climb high escarpments. Perhaps that explained why her son had never been disturbed by Elizabeth's long walks.

After a steep but brief climb, the path became wider and almost level. Mr. Darcy waited for her to reach him, then walked by her side. "I hope I am not going too quickly for you."

"Not at all. The climb is invigorating. You are fortunate to live in a region where such hills and views abound. The ones in Hertfordshire, alas, are but pale imitations."

"Hertfordshire has other riches – fertile land and lovely gardens, among others. The rocky soil here is less forgiving to those who must make their living from it." He gestured towards a break in the rocks through which the view of a wide valley was visible. "If you look through there, you will see the River Wye. It joins the River Derwent just south of us."

Elizabeth paused to examine the view. It took her a moment to find the winding trail of the river, visible more by the trees lining its edge than the water itself. "You must know this place well after visiting it so often."

"Yes, my parents brought me here even as a young child. We would picnic not far from where your aunt and uncle set up their meal, though we would climb the tor first. My father would tease my mother, saying she would stay up there forever if hunger did not drive her down."

"He must have been very fond of her to have established the tradition of coming here in her memory."

"He was." Darcy looked off into the distance, then began walking beside her again. "Their bond was...exceptional."

This was a potentially dangerous subject given her history with Mr. Darcy, but Elizabeth found herself inexplicably curious about his parents. Perhaps it was the affection with which he spoke of them. "How did they meet? Was it an arranged marriage?"

"It was not arranged at all; quite the contrary, as it disrupted other arrangements. They first met as children when my father's family visited hers. My mother announced her decision to marry my father at the advanced age of four, and continued to insist on it for some years afterward, even though she did not see him again until much later."

Elizabeth laughed. "He must have made quite an impression upon her!"

"You might say so. Depending on which of them was telling the story, he saved her from either drowning, a beating, or both – though I never understood how she could have been beaten if she had already drowned. She apparently still received the beating, but it was several years later when her father told her he had heard quite enough of this nonsense about her marrying James Darcy; *he* would be the one to decide whom she would marry, and James Darcy was not even on the list of possibilities. Apparently she was not easily convinced, even at ten years of age."

"A young lady of strong will! What did your father think of this?"

"He knew nothing of it. To him she was just the little girl he had fished out of the pond and saved from a beating by taking the blame for the entire episode himself, even though he had been nowhere near her when she decided to pretend to be a fish."

"How chivalrous of him!"

"He claims he felt sorry for her since she was so frightened, and one beating more or less made no difference to him. He was no stranger to beatings, having a strong will of his own – as she discovered much later."

"After they were safely married, no doubt?"

Darcy laughed, and suddenly he looked years younger. "No, it was much earlier – the day after they met again as adults, when she pointed out to him all the reasons why she could not marry him, and he simply went on planning for it."

Elizabeth's eyebrows shot up. "He did not accept her refusal?" she said with some indignation.

With a sidelong glance, Darcy said, "Well, it was not so much a matter of her being unwilling, but of circumstances not permitting it."

"But if she refused, he should have listened to her!" Too late Elizabeth realized that refusal of offers of marriage was the last topic which she should discuss with him.

Darcy remained silent for a moment, then said, "Tell me, when your aunt and uncle gave their reasons why you could not climb the rocks here, did it make you stop wishing to do it?"

"Of course not, but I did *not* tell them I was going to do it in spite of what they said."

"Still, I imagine you tried to think of ways to get around their interdiction."

"Yes, but I did not insist on having my own way!"

He paused, his lips tightening, and shook his head. "I am not explaining this well. Perhaps I should start at the beginning."

Part II

London,
1781

"Darcy! Can you spare me a minute?" Lieutenant Francis Fitzwilliam hailed the young man in the blue uniform of the Horse Guards.

James Darcy removed his tasselled headgear with a sigh of relief. No matter how splendid its appearance, the helmet was far too heavy for comfort. "No, I would rather continue to march in step for another two hours than to speak to you. Of course I have time!"

"Excellent. I have a favor to ask of you."

"Oh, no." James waggled a finger at his friend. "The last time I agreed to do you a favor, I ended up on punishment detail for a fortnight for covering your absence while you met with that girl!"

"Yes, and I have apologized for that at *least* a hundred times. This is nothing like that, though. *You* get to meet the girl, and no regulations are broken."

"I fail to see how that could qualify as doing you a favor," said James warily.

Lieutenant Fitzwilliam laughed. "It is very simple. I want you to go to Lord Montalban's ball and dance with my sister."

James gave him a suspicious look. "What is wrong with your sister that you have to ask your friends to dance with her?"

"Nothing is wrong with her! Well..." He leaned closer to James and said in a confidential manner, "She is tall. Almost as tall as me. Taller than half the men at any ball, so they do not ask her to dance. Since she is rarely asked to dance, the other men decide she must be a wallflower. Her Season is not going well, and since it is important for her to be well established in society this year, my great-aunt – the one who is sponsoring her – asked me to find some tall friends to dance with her."

"Are you certain that is the only reason? She does not have foul breath or a harelip, and she will not step all over my feet during the dance?"

"Of course not. She is perfectly presentable apart from her height. You have seen her before – she is the one you fished from the pond – so you know there's no harelip."

"She did not seem particularly tall to me then," said Darcy dubiously.

"Of course she was not tall then! She was only a child. Look at it this way – will it not be pleasant to dance with a woman whom you do not tower over? You will be able to see her face, not just the top of her head."

"Very well. I will come, if you can get me an invitation, and I will dance with your sister." Darcy vaguely remembered the little girl, and tried to imagine her as a young lady. She was likely to be quite plain, but he would dance with her for his friend's sake.

Lord and Lady Montalban's ball was one of the most anticipated events of the Season. The cost of the hot-house flowers and wax candles alone could have fed half the beggars in London, but there was no denying it was an impressive spectacle. James Darcy made an unsuccessful circuit of the ballroom in search of Francis Fitzwilliam, taking care to get a good look at the wallflowers as he went. There were two possibilities for Francis's sister – both tall, one with a face that was more interesting than beautiful, and one who appeared rather sickly and as if she would rather be somewhere else. James hoped that the one with the interesting face would turn out to be Francis's sister, but until Francis put in an appearance to introduce him, James could only dance with ladies he had met on other occasions.

Married women were usually the best possibilities for an enjoyable dance. They were always pleased to be asked, even by a second son with no prospects, and he could enjoy flirting with them without fear that they might take it too seriously. Dancing was supposed to be fun, after all.

Mrs. Alston was happy to accept his invitation to dance. As they made their way down the line of dancers, he noticed several new debutantes in their white dresses, some pretending to experience they clearly did not possess, and others not appearing old enough to be out of the schoolroom. One of them caught his eye as he passed by, not so much for her beauty as for the liveliness of her expression and the energy she brought to her dancing. Her face would never be the toast of the town, but unlike many of the others, she looked as if she were enjoying herself. He found himself watching her as she in turn moved down the line with her partner. Her musical laughter rippled past him as she tapped her feet to the music when it was her turn to wait out.

The pity of it was that James could not ask her to dance until they had been introduced, and it would be difficult to ask for an introduction until he discovered her name. Mrs. Alston did not know her, so instead James asked the attractive daughter of the Prussian ambassador for the next set. Miss Hoemke was more of an age with the unknown young lady and therefore more likely to be acquainted with her, but their dance was a lively one that precluded much opportunity for conversation.

Francis finally arrived towards the end of the set. James's next course of action was clear; he would dance with his friend's sister. If she also did not know the lively young lady, he would seek out Lady Montalban to request an introduction. Then he could discover if her conversation was as enchanting as the rest of her. If it was, he might be in serious danger.

Francis was waiting for him when the dance ended. "Glad to see you made it," he said. "Shall I introduce you to my sister?"

"That is why I came here," said James cheerfully, "although I now have another reason. I think I have fallen in love."

"Anyone I know?"

"*I* do not even know her. She is over by the windows, standing with Sir Charles Granding and his wife."

Francis gave him an odd look. "The one with dark hair and gold trim on her white dress?"

"Yes, that one. Charming, isn't she? Do you know her?"

"Yes," he said, dragging out the word as if reluctant to end it. "You might say I know her. That is Anne."

James turned to him in shock. "Your *sister*? *That* is little Annie whom I fished out of the pond?"

"*That* is Lady Anne to you, and I strongly advise against falling in love with her." He did not need to give a reason; everyone knew an earl's daughter could do much better than a penniless second son from an untitled family. "Come, I will introduce you, and you can get this dance over with."

James felt a heaviness in his stomach. It was a pity that his heart and body seemed to think Lady Anne's social position was irrelevant to their condition. Something deep inside him kept insisting she was meant to be his, or perhaps that *he* was meant to be *hers*; he was not quite sure which it was, or if it mattered. What did matter was that he became more entranced with every step he took in her direction.

She greeted her brother affectionately, with a smile that lit her eyes as well as her face. "You came! I thought you might have forgotten."

"How could I forget with all the reminders you sent me?" Francis teased her. "But I have a friend who has requested an introduction to you. May I present to your acquaintance – or perhaps I should say to your *re*-acquaintance – my friend and comrade in arms, Lieutenant Darcy."

James bowed, but she did not look in his direction. Instead she glared at her brother, her lips tight. "Francis, I cannot believe you did this! Have you no shame?"

Her unexpected and inexplicable anger felt like a blow to James's chest. Why should she wish to avoid his acquaintance? "Lady Anne, I fear you must have confused me with someone else. I assure you I am perfectly respectable."

Her expression softened a little as she finally looked at him. "My deepest apologies, Lieutenant Darcy. I know of nothing to your discredit, and I am pleased to meet you. My brother is a meddler and a troublemaker, that is all."

Francis was laughing. "And I *believed* you when you said you remembered nothing of it! Oh, Anne, you wicked girl!"

"You stop that, Francis Fitzwilliam! It is not at all humorous." But a smile tugged at her lips even as she said it.

"Pardon me," said James, "but is there something I am supposed to know? Because I can assure you I am quite in the dark."

"It is just one of those silly matters that brothers and sisters tease each other about when they are young," she said. "I would say it is of no importance, but since I know Francis can hardly wait to have you to himself so that he can tell you everything, I will relate it myself."

Francis said, "He does remember fishing you out of the pond."

"I do, but not at all to your discredit," James assured her. "I remember it because, like all ten year old boys, I longed to be a hero, and at the time I felt I had done something heroic – so I thank you for that happy moment." He bowed again.

"You were very kind. The matter my brother is so enjoying teasing me about came afterwards when, in the way of all four year old girls, I became enamored of my hero, and I told my family that I intended to marry him when I grew up. See, it is nothing so awful, Francis; I can admit to it myself."

Chuckling, Francis said, "She is leaving out an important part, wherein she announced this at regular intervals for some years afterwards!"

Noting the flush rising in Lady Anne's cheeks, James said, "Why, I believe that is the nicest compliment I have ever received. What a pity for me you changed your mind! I promise you, Lady Anne, that all you need do is to say but one word, or give one glance, and I will go down on my knees here and now and beg for your hand. But until you decide to say that word, will you take mercy on your once-upon-a-time almost-betrothed and grant me the honor of being your partner for the next set?"

"I would be delighted, Lieutenant Darcy, *especially* if it means we can leave my annoying brother behind." She offered him her hand.

A shock of warmth ran up his arm as he took it. Could she hear his heart pounding as he led her to the line of dancers? Francis had been right about one thing; it was pleasant to be able to see his partner's face, especially when her eyes sparkled like stars on a dark night.

"I do apologize for that little scene," she said softly. "I should not let Francis's teasing bother me so, even if he does enjoy embarrassing me."

"I am sorry he embarrassed you. If it is any consolation, he is going to embarrass *me* far more the next time he speaks to you, when he will no doubt repeat certain unguarded things I said to him earlier tonight – and *I* do not have the excuse of extreme youth."

She tilted her head, smiling. "This sounds serious."

"It is. Very serious." He leveled his voice. "I would not ordinarily tell you this, but like you, I would rather you heard it from me than from Francis. I had been watching you dance tonight, though I did not recognize the lovely young lady as the bedraggled four year old girl I once met. When Francis arrived, I told him I was falling in love, and asked if he knew your name."

The musicians began to play, relieving her of the need to make an immediate response, but even in the candlelight he could see her cheeks were covered with the deepest blush. As they moved through the stately patterns of the minuet, she said carefully, "Gentlemen will have their jests."

"I was not jesting." What in God's name had inspired him to say that?

She crossed in front of him in the dance, a crease of annoyance appearing between her brows. "I find this difficult to credit. Tell me, Lieutenant, how did my brother convince you to play this role?"

"He has nothing to do with this. I am making a fool of myself without help from anyone." He could see his words were disturbing her. What could he do to recover the moment? "Perhaps now that we have exhausted the various types of ammunition in your brother's arsenal, we can return to more traditional topics of conversation, such as how Lady Montalban was able to find such a copious number of flowers at this season. I had not realized there were enough hothouses in England to produce so many blossoms."

She seemed to relax a little. "It is rather impressive. I was admiring the roses earlier. Hothouse blooms, it is true, but they are still a promise of summer to come."

So she was fond of roses. James tucked away the knowledge. He could tell Lady Anne was no hothouse bloom, unlike many of the other young ladies at the ball. She made her opinions known, and he liked that. Now he needed to persuade her to be of the opinion she wanted him to partner her for the supper dance. That would give them more time for conversation – and for him to discover whether his instincts were right.

"The flowers you sent this morning are lovely, Lieutenant. I thank you for them. I am very partial to roses," said Lady Anne when James called upon her the following day. She meant it; unlike the noted beauties of the Season who were deluged with bouquets the day after a ball, it was rare for her to receive one, much less her favorite flowers. The sitting rooms of the noted beauties would be filled with admirers today. She would only have the one, so she proposed walking in Hyde Park to avoid the prospect of stilted conversation in the presence of her great-aunt.

He offered her his arm as soon as they reached the street. "Dancing with you last night brought me great pleasure. If the flowers conveyed even an iota of that to you, I am well satisfied."

She set her hand lightly on his arm. It had not been her imagination at the ball; there was something about touching him that made her feel as if she had been only half-alive until that moment. Still, she needed to be cautious. Just because she found him attractive did not mean he was sincere in his admiration of her. "It was a very enjoyable ball, though I remain puzzled by certain parts of it."

"Puzzled? What part of the ball was puzzling?"

"I am puzzled by your attentions to me. I can come up with no reason for it except that you might have done it on Francis's behalf, as some sort of prank."

James looked charmingly guilty, and Anne's heart twisted at what it might mean. "I should make a small confession. Francis did ask me to dance with you, but that was before the ball. Once I had seen you, I wanted to dance with you even before I knew you were his sister."

"And before you knew I was the daughter of an Earl? You are aware, I hope, that I have no dowry to speak of, despite my rank," she said abruptly. If his interest lay in her fortune, she would rather know it now.

His smile widened. "I was unaware of that, but I consider it happy news. I would not wish my attentions to you to be misconstrued. I am not a fortune-hunter."

That was not the answer she had expected. "In any case, it would make no difference. My brother has apparently been remiss in passing along information. I suppose you are also unaware my betrothal was arranged years ago, before I was even out of the schoolroom."

A furrow formed between his brows as he looked down at her, his smile fading. "No. I did not know that."

To her surprise, he seemed truly disturbed by this intelligence. She tightened her hand on his arm in a brief moment of sympathy. He had been kind to her, and had matters fallen out differently, he was just the sort of man she might like. "I am sorry to disappoint any hopes, but those are the facts of the matter."

"This cannot have been your idea, if you were still in the schoolroom," he said.

"Of course not. It is an alliance of sorts arranged by my father."

His lips were in a thin line. "Are you attached to him?"

She deliberately misunderstood him. "My father?"

"No. The man he chose for you."

"I fail to see what difference it makes, but I have met him only twice."

"Who is he?" he asked bluntly, his manner a sharp contrast to his earlier politeness.

She looked away toward the blue waters of the Serpentine. "I would prefer not to give his name at the moment. I doubt you know him."

"Are you ashamed of him?"

"No, of course not! I am merely worried you might do something rash; that is all. You can discover his name easily enough if you so choose." This was beginning to make her nervous. Why could he not say the appropriate polite words about how fortunate her betrothed was?

"Well, I *am* going to do something many people might describe as rash, and that is to try to convince you not to marry him." At Anne's horror-struck look, he added more gently, "And yes, I do recognize that whoever your father has chosen for you is no doubt a much better match than I am, but it will not stop me from trying."

She laughed, even though part of her wanted to cry. "I do not know which part of your presumption is greater; that you would disregard my father's plans for me, or that you would be speaking of marriage the day after we met."

He leaned down and spoke quietly in her ear. "I spoke of marriage yesterday as well. You may not have taken me seriously, but that does not preclude the possibility I meant it."

A shiver ran down her spine as his warm breath tickled her ear and neck. She had never been one to flirt thoughtlessly, but something about his intensity was difficult to ignore. Striving to ease the tension, she said lightly, "I could understand your reasons to move quickly if I were an heiress or well-dowered, but as that is not the case, I do have to question your judgement in pursuing *me* so eagerly on such short acquaintance."

His smile returned, something which relieved her more than she cared to admit. "I could plead that I have known you for over a decade, but it would be misleading. No, although I am embarrassed to admit it, this is just my fate as a Darcy. A family tradition, if you will."

"A family tradition?" she said with a laugh.

"Yes, to fall in love quickly and irrevocably. My father warned me that men of our family always recognize these things immediately, and are loyal ever afterwards. He proposed to my mother the night they met. My brother was slow about it, waiting a full four days to propose to his wife. My father claimed it was our destiny, like it or not." He frowned. "Unfortunately, he did *not* tell me what to do if it turned out I was not an adequate match for the lady in question or if she were engaged to someone else – so, as you see, I was telling the truth last night when I said it was a pity you had changed your mind about marrying me. Obviously it was a failure of foresight on my part not to have proposed to you when you were four."

His combination of flirtation and cheerful nonsense made her insides feel oddly light. "It would have done you no good. Even when I was four, my father was furious whenever I said I was going to marry you. He forbade me to so much as mention your name."

He blinked in surprise. "Good Lord, what did I ever do to make your father think so ill of me?"

"Nothing. Being a younger son without a fortune of your own is all it took to disqualify you as a potential suitor." There was no point in mentioning her own frequent adoring references to him had annoyed her father more than anything.

"That is a crime of which I am without doubt guilty," James said seriously. "It is a problem I must address. I cannot provide for a wife on a Lieutenant's salary. In a few years, when a particular living at my brother's disposal becomes vacant, I will be selling out; and I always thought that would be the time to consider marriage. I did not anticipate meeting you now, or that you would be the daughter of a peer. Until last night, I believed my father had imagined all that nonsense about the fate of Darcy men. It is somewhat sobering to discover I was mistaken."

"Lieutenant Darcy," she said with amusement, "this is all very flattering, but did you not hear a word I said earlier? I am marrying another man."

His charming smile brightened his face once again. "I heard you perfectly well. I simply did not accept it."

"It is not up to you whether to accept it or not!" she snapped. If only he would stop pretending she had a choice in the matter. Did he suppose she *liked* the idea of being married off like some sort of chattel?

He halted and turned to look at her, laying his free hand on hers as it rested on his arm. "Lady Anne, I cannot and will not stop you from marrying him if that is what you truly desire, but I also must act on what I know in my heart to be right. I do not know how to explain it, but have you never experienced the sense that something *must* be done, regardless of what difficulties stand in your way?"

"My family would tell you I experience that far too often!"

"Then you know what I mean. I would be very curious, I must admit, as to what sort of thing you might have felt you had to do."

It would be a particularly poor idea to tell him that for many years she would have said she could marry no one but James Darcy. Instead she said, "It is most often some unladylike behavior of which my family disapproves. And you? What other things speak to your heart?"

"Various things. I cannot bear to see an animal misused, and I have been known to come to blows with opponents who outnumber me over it, but righting a wrong is hardly the same thing as this." He paused to think, his eyes distant. "It is likely a poor example, and may make no sense to you at all. You are, I assume, familiar with the Vale of Matlock?"

She raised an eyebrow. "Of course. It is not that far from Charlton House."

"Then you would recognize the Black Rocks that rise above the valley."

"Naturally." Her heart began to pound.

He took a deep breath, as if about to confess some deep secret. "When I pass them and see the stone pillars rising into the sky, looking like some sort of sacred monuments built by giants, I know I must climb to the top of them and stand looking out over the valley, my arms outstretched as if I could fly. Not necessarily that day or even that month, but they will keep calling me until I do it. There; now you may laugh at me if you wish." His serious tone reverted to light flirtation at the end.

Anne felt no impulse to laugh. All she could do was to stare at him. Could he tell it was suddenly hard for her to breathe?

"What is the matter?" said Lieutenant Darcy anxiously. "Do you dislike heights? There would be no reason for *you* to climb the rocks unless you wished to do so."

She shook her head slowly, her eyes fixed on his. "I am not afraid of heights. I love to be high in the air. My brothers once took me to the Black Rocks and dared me to climb them, but there was no need of a dare, since I wanted nothing more than to reach the top as soon as I could. It is one of my happiest memories. I begged for years to be taken there again, but they said it was inappropriate for a young lady."

His eyes grew suddenly darker. Very softly he said, "I knew you were the one."

Lady Anne Fitzwilliam knew foolishness when she heard it. What did it signify, after all, that they both liked the Black Rocks? The spot was well-known for its beauty and appeared with some regularity in engravings. She had even seen it once in a painting. If the Black Rocks were not as popular an attraction as Dovedale, they were still a common stop for travellers making a tour of the Peak. If all those artists and travellers admired them for their beauty, why should it be so surprising that both she and Lieutenant James Darcy would appreciate the spot as well?

Likewise, it hardly constituted a recommendation that a child of four had fallen into hero-worship of an older boy she barely knew. It was more the *idea* of James Darcy she had loved than the actual boy. He had helped her out of the pond and then taken a beating for her sake, something her brothers would never have done, but it really had been a bit foolish of him once she considered it. She had deserved that beating for running away from her nursemaid and venturing into the forbidden pond.

Then there was the matter of his ridiculous family tradition. Dependable men did not fall in love with a woman on a moment's notice. It was nothing but an excuse to try to win her favor, a seducer's trick. Men did that sort of thing all the time. He had no doubt already known he was perfectly safe in speaking to her of marriage since she was promised to another.

Yes, Lady Anne Fitzwilliam knew foolishness when she heard it – and all of those arguments she had carefully constructed were foolish. None of those reasons mattered. He had spoken words that had reached straight to her heart, and when she looked into his eyes, she knew he was right. She *was* the one for him, and *he* was the only one for her, even if anyone else would have said he looked vaguely ridiculous attempting to determine how he could support a wife he could not obtain. She had seen the perplexity in his dark eyes as he wondered at himself for even considering it. He never claimed he was happy to be hopelessly in love with her; he seemed rather to see it as a problem, which in fact it was. Just one of those unfortunate things that happen in life, like being a penniless second son, or having the misfortune to fall in love with a woman he could not have – or being betrothed to a stranger because of her father's inability to live within his income.

Most likely James would have the good sense to talk himself out of the entire conceit once he was back at his barracks. Everything he said might have been true, but what was the point in fighting for something he could never have? He would do better to attempt to forget her and move on with his life, and she should be grateful that for one day she had an admirer just like all the other young ladies, the ones without the misfortune of being too tall and lacking the requisite fascination with nothing beyond the next ball. It had been lovely to have James Darcy look at her as if his entire future rested in her eyes, and no doubt the memory would give her comfort in the future. It would be for the best if they did not meet again. But if he did not call again, or if he strolled past her at the next soiree with some pretty young thing on his arm, she knew she would cry herself to sleep.

Fate had played a cruel trick on both of them.

She knew better than to allow herself to hope to see him again. Hopes like that always led to disappointment. They had danced together twice and walked in Hyde Park the next day, and that was all. There was no future for them, and it would be best if he realized that from the start, before it became even harder to part. Better a small pain now than a larger one later (even if a small voice within her jeered that this was hardly a small pain). At the next ball, she would not look for him nor compare any dance partner she was fortunate enough to obtain to him. The Season had only two more months to run, and then she would be returning to Matlock while James would be required to stay with his regiment in London. The next time she returned to Town would be to purchase her bridal clothes. Two months was such a short time that it barely mattered whether she saw him again or not.

Which was why, when he called on her again the next morning, she burst into tears instead of greeting him politely.

Fortunately, her great-aunt was out paying morning calls of her own, from which Anne had excused herself owing to an imaginary headache, so there was no one to comment on this extraordinary display. Nor was there anyone to witness when Lieutenant Darcy took the natural step of enclosing her in his arms to offer her comfort, nor when *that* natural step led to the *next* natural step which occurs between embracing couples who are powerfully attracted to one another.

That state of affairs might have persisted for some time were it not for the clatter of a dropped tea tray just outside the door, which led to the further natural step of the two of them jumping as far apart as possible within a small room and attempting to appear innocent and virtuous while managing to look thoroughly guilty. Fortunately for them, the sympathetic maidservant blamed the entire disaster on her own clumsiness, after which the Lieutenant insisted on personally informing the housekeeper that the tea tray incident was solely *his* fault and had occurred only because of his own carelessness in stretching his legs in the wrong place and causing the maid to trip. The housekeeper, after one glance at the red eyes and disarrayed hair of Lady Anne, condescended to accept this unlikely tale and told the Lieutenant sternly to be more careful where he stretched his legs in the future, which he solemnly promised to do.

Having escaped disaster by a hair, the two decided another walk in the park was their wisest course. Once they made their escape, Lieutenant Darcy said, "I can guess who is the favorite member of your family below stairs."

"There is no competition for the title. My sister delights in criticizing the staff, even when they have done nothing wrong."

"Even without that, I heartily agree with the staff. But you have not yet told me what caused you such distress when I arrived. Had you received ill tidings? Is there anything I can do to help?"

Lady Anne looked down to hide her blushes. "No. I was afraid you would not return and I would never see you again."

"Why would you think that? I told you I intended to marry you, which would be very difficult if I never saw you again."

"And *I* told you I could not, so what was the point in returning?"

He drew her a little closer to his side. "My foolish love, there are reasons by the score for me to return. Even if I could make myself stay away, which I cannot, I have not given up hope. King Henry did not give up hope before Agincourt when facing impossible odds. Five years ago, did we not laugh at the idea of the American colonists winning their independence? Yet I think it unlikely any of us will be surprised now if they do prevail."

"Those are military matters," she said despairingly. "It would be easier to triumph over an army than over my father."

They walked in silence for a few minutes, and then he said soberly, "Do you wish me to leave?"

She could not look at him, but she shook her head, swallowing hard. Bursting into tears in her sitting room was bad enough; doing it again in the middle of Hyde Park would be mortifying.

"Then I will not believe it is hopeless." When she failed to reply, he said, "Is something the matter?"

Squaring her shoulders, she said in a trembling voice, "I will have you know that I *never* cry. Never."

He drew her a little closer, then led her down a path into a stand of trees that offered some slight privacy. "Of course not," he said warmly. "Fresh air can make anyone's eyes water."

She folded her hand into a fist and struck his arm lightly, just as she might have done to Francis. "You are horrible," she informed him.

Leaning toward her, he stole a brief kiss. "And there is one victory I have already won – I am the first man you kissed."

"You won that battle fifteen years ago!"

He laughed. "That is true, though I had quite forgotten it until this moment. George and Francis teased me about it abominably."

"And my nursemaid scolded me for half an hour about proper behavior. I could not see why there was a problem, since I had already decided to marry you."

That statement naturally required another kiss. It was some time later that James said, "But I do wish to hear more about why you were promised to this man. I assume your father must have strong reasons to have arranged it when you were so young." His stubborn expression told her he was only gathering information for use at a later date.

She feared that if she tried to explain it gradually, she would start to cry again, so she simply blurted it out. "It was the only way to save our home."

Clearly that was not what he had expected. "I do not understand."

"My father was – and still is – deeply in debt. One of his bankers desperately wants to be accepted into the *ton*, but his money is from trade. If he were married to an Earl's daughter, though, he could not be ignored. I do not know the precise details, but he holds the deed to Charlton House now, and will return it to my father after I marry him – or evict him if I do not. My father was very happy to take the bargain."

"He sold you," he said darkly.

"I do not wish to see my family lose its ancestral home either," she said defensively. "So it was decided I was to have one Season to become established in the *ton,* and then we will marry at the beginning of next Season, in front of as many of the *ton* as can be convinced to attend."

"So soon?" Lieutenant Darcy chewed his lower lip. "I had hoped for more time, and it seems unlikely your father will be easily convinced to change his mind."

"Impossible," said Lady Anne, her voice trembling. Until yesterday, the prospect of marrying Mr. Berg, while not something she anticipated with pleasure, had not seemed particularly upsetting; but now everything had changed. "I have no choice."

"No choice but to pay with your life for the sins your father committed! It is unacceptable."

"It is inevitable." She did not want to argue with him. Why could they not speak of pleasant things and pretend for a few minutes they might have a future? That way she might have a chance of keeping her composure. He would not think so well of her if she turned into a watering pot whenever he saw her.

"I am not willing to accept that. It is a difficult situation without question, but nothing is impossible if it is what we both want. We just need to consider the options – perhaps arranging for your intended to be caught in a compromising position with a young lady from a very demanding family? If nothing else..." He stopped and shook his head.

"What?" she asked with a certain dread.

"I should not have said anything – but if all else fails, there is Gretna Green. It is not what I would want for you, but it would be preferable to giving you up."

"How could I run off with you, knowing it means my family will lose their home? That my sister will never have the chance of a Season? If it were just a matter of my reputation, it would be difficult enough, but as it is, my entire family would pay dearly for my choice."

His brows drew together and he placed his hand over hers. "I am sorry. I did not mean to cause you distress; that is the last thing I would want. When I have a problem, I try to think through it by speaking it aloud, but I see I have taken it too far. I will not press you further, but I have not given up. I plan to write to my brother for advice. Perhaps he will be able to see something I cannot."

"What if he tells my father?" asked Anne anxiously.

"There is no need to worry. I will tell him it is a secret, and he will keep it. He understands the tradition."

"The two of you are friends as well as brothers?"

The Lieutenant gave her a sunny smile. "Oh, yes. We have always been close – to the chagrin of some of my other friends."

"Why would it trouble them?"

"Apparently they think I should resent George for being heir to my father's estates, and he is supposed to begrudge every farthing he gives me. But I do not resent him, and he is very generous with me. I rescued him once when we were at Cambridge, and one of my friends said I should have let him fall to his death instead so I would inherit. Stuff and nonsense – as if I could ever be happy that way!"

"You seem to make a habit of coming to the rescue! How did you save *him*? I assume you did not have to fish him out of a pond."

"No, this was mere foolishness. He was foxed, and accepted a bet to walk along the ledge outside our window. We were on the top floor, but the ledge was wide enough until George looked down and became dizzy. He lost his balance and was clinging to the ledge by his fingers, out of reach of any of us. I ran down to the room below ours and went out the window, then climbed up to George until he could put his feet on my shoulders. It was an old stone building, easy enough to clamber up for someone with no fear of heights. George would have been in no danger except that there was ivy covering the rocks there, and he was not sober enough to work around it. Nothing dramatic, apart from a rather embarrassing scene I interrupted in the room below when I went in without knocking." He grinned at her.

"How much older than you is he?"

"George? About a quarter of an hour."

"No, I mean – oh, are you twins?"

"In the flesh." He bowed to her. "But we do not look alike. You would have no difficulty telling us apart."

"Especially if you were both atop the Black Rocks – you would be the one standing on the edge while he told you to come down."

"That is another way to tell us apart," he agreed. "Look for the one who turns green at the edge of a cliff, and that is George."

Soon everyone in the *ton* was aware Lieutenant Darcy could be expected to be in constant attendance on Lady Anne Fitzwilliam. When it was seen Lady Anne did nothing in particular to encourage him, no one thought anything of it beyond that it was sweet the tall, handsome Lieutenant should be so devoted to a woman he could never win.

During the fashionable hour, he could be seen driving Lady Anne through Hyde Park. At any ball, he would be certain to claim the dinner dance; and he was her escort at a series of soirees and Venetian breakfasts around town. Their stolen kisses, confidences and letters were well hidden from view, as were Lieutenant Darcy's increasingly desperate plans to rescue Lady Anne from her engagement.

By the end of a month, Lieutenant Darcy had paid enough calls at the Matlock townhouse to be recognized immediately by much of the staff. He was surprised when the butler frowned on seeing him when he opened the door one day. Although it was superfluous under the circumstances, he handed the butler his card and requested the privilege of seeing Lady Anne.

"Sir, I am sorry to say I have been given orders not to admit you today or any other day."

James stiffened as if he had been slapped. "Lady Anne does not wish to see me?" he asked, his throat tight.

The butler looked at him with some sympathy. "I am not at liberty to say who gave me the orders."

"Not Lady Anne, then?" It felt like he could breathe again.

Pursing his lips, the butler said carefully, "Lady Anne's father is a cautious man."

"Matlock is here?" That was an unexpected blow. He had thought Matlock planned to stay in the North where no one could call in his debts.

"His lordship arrived yesterday, sir."

"That would be it, then," James said darkly. "He wants to keep us apart. Is Lady Anne aware of your orders?"

"I cannot say what her ladyship knows, but she appears to be expecting you."

James swore under his breath. "So it is to look as if I have abandoned her. Damn him! Does he not realize it will hurt her more that way?" He was not as much speaking to the butler as to himself. The butler had been far more forthcoming to him than he needed to be, and he should be grateful for that small mercy.

There was nothing to be done for it now. Later he could find Francis and ask him to explain to Anne why he had not called, and James would haunt every social event until he crossed paths with her. Lord Matlock could not prevent him from approaching her in public, after all. "Thank you for your assistance," he said dully.

The butler watched the dejected Lieutenant walk away. He was fond of Lady Anne, and the Lieutenant had always been pleasant and gracious to him, unlike many of the gentlemen he encountered. He walked slowly to the sitting room where Lady Anne was reading a book.

She looked up at him hopefully. "Is Lieutenant Darcy here?"

"Your ladyship, I pride myself on following my instructions from your father, which sometimes might preclude informing a family member of events of importance to them. It is my hope that your ladyship's sensibilities would not be injured by any such actions of mine."

She snapped her book closed. "What are you trying to tell me, Simons?"

He paused. "In such a circumstance, I would not be able to tell you anything since I had been forbidden to do so. But if it were to happen that one of your acquaintances did not visit you as expected, it might be worth considering whether there were any obstacles placed in that acquaintance's way, rather than to assume your acquaintance had lost interest."

Frowning, she tapped her foot. "I assume, then, that it is unlikely Lieutenant Darcy will be calling on me today."

"I would call it highly unlikely, your ladyship."

"Or tomorrow, or next week?"

"Equally unlikely."

She paced restlessly to the window, then turned back to the butler and spoke decisively. "Simons, the two footmen who accompany me when I go out – do they report to my father?"

"That is part of their duties, my lady. The same applies to any excursions Lady Catherine might take. Naturally, if they were escorting *her* on some errand when *you* wished to go out, we would arrange for other footmen to accompany you."

"I see." Her lips were set in a firm line.

"Will there be anything else, my lady?"

"Nothing at present. And Simons – I thank you for your consideration."

He bowed. "It is my honor to serve you."

James returned to the barracks to find a stilted letter from Matlock's secretary awaiting him. It coldly informed him that if he attempted to dance with Lady Anne or even to speak to her at a social gathering, she would be forbidden to leave the house. The magistrate would be called if he was spotted in the environs of Matlock House. He ripped it to pieces, swearing the entire time in an uncharacteristic fit of temper. It was but a fortnight until Anne was to leave London. Was he not even to have the chance of seeing her again?

Francis Fitzwilliam told him apologetically he could do nothing to help. "He knows we are friends. He made it clear someone would be watching every step I take when I am with her. If I thought it would help, I would still try, but Anne would be the one to pay the price if I am caught."

Growing too desperate to care about propriety, James finally called on an old friend who was not in the Life Guards. The following day, his friend reported his mission accomplished. "She says Hyde Park, your special place, at mid-day, but it may be several days before she can come there safely."

It was three agonizingly long days before she appeared, her face wan as she glanced back over her shoulder. She could not stay long, she warned him; and James broke his promise to himself and begged her to elope with him. She was in tears and he was near that point himself by the time she said she had to leave.

Anne had thought it would be easier when she returned to Derbyshire for the summer. In London everything had reminded her of James – places they had walked together, houses where they had danced together. A horse of that certain chestnut color would cross her path, and her eyes would immediately swivel to see who rode it. The sight of an officer in the uniform of the Life Guards could bring tears to her eyes.

There were no such reminders in Derbyshire, apart from the pond where he had rescued her all those years ago, even though they had been almost two different people when that happened. But she had spent years there telling herself stories of how she would marry James Darcy when she grew up, and she had practiced the name 'Lady Anne Darcy' often enough that it felt like her own. Even after her father had forbidden her as a girl to mention his name, she still thought of him as hers. She only stopped mentioning her plans aloud. James Darcy pervaded her every childhood memory.

She missed him fiercely. Late at night she would dream of running off with him, knowing it could never happen, but wishing for it so hard that her heart ached. She lived for the letters from Francis which invariably said it was business as usual at the barracks. James had said that would be the code to tell her he loved her.

When a footman unexpectedly announced Lieutenant Darcy's arrival to her, she almost did not believe her ears, but it was true. The servants at Matlock had never received instructions to refuse him entry, since he was two days' journey away in London. A sheer rush of delight filled her – at least until she actually saw him.

James looked terrible. His expression was tight and miserable, his hair tousled and disarranged, his coat spattered with mud, and the knot in his cravat barely deserved the name. For a moment she thought their separation must have affected him even more badly than she had feared, but then she realized he had not smiled at her.

"What is the matter?" she asked, taking his hands in hers.

He shook his head. "I am sorry," he said hoarsely. "I know I should not have come here, but I had to see you. I could not...could not go..."

She had never seen him like this. "You are unwell. I pray you, sit down and tell me what has happened."

But he did not take the spot on the sofa beside her that she had indicated. Instead, he fell to his knees and let his head sink onto her lap like a child in search of comfort.

Now truly alarmed, she said, "James, you must tell me what has happened." Her hands reached out to stroke his hair. "What is the matter?"

He stiffened for a moment, but said nothing. Instead he pulled out a crumpled sheet of paper and pushed it into her hand. Unfolding it, she saw it was a letter from the steward at Pemberley. A sick feeling filled her stomach as the words swam before her eyes. *Terrible tragedy during the night...your brother and his wife both overcome by smoke...several of the staff perished with them...little structural damage but all the contents of several rooms destroyed...request your immediate return and further instructions.*

Without a second thought, she wrapped her arms around him. "Oh, James, I am so very sorry – so grieved for you. What a terrible loss, and so unexpected!" When his breathing became ragged, she said softly, "I am here, dearest." Poor James!

He adored his brother... *had* adored his brother, his twin, his only remaining family.

"What is this?" roared Lord Matlock. He stood in the doorway, breathing heavily. No doubt one of the servants had fetched him.

"This is not what it seems, sir," said Anne soothingly. "Lieutenant Darcy has received tragic news."

"He will receive tragic news from me if he ever comes near you again!" He gestured to a footman. "Throw him out and do not allow him to return."

"You do not understand!" exclaimed Anne, stepping between James and her father. "I pray you, listen to me."

James rose to his feet, his face void of any expression. "You need not bother," he said to the footman, his voice hollow. "I will leave. Lady Anne, pray accept my thanks for your kindness." He turned and walked out of the room, looking back only once.

"James!" she cried, but her father grabbed her arms and would not allow her to go after him. "Oh, James," she said softly, almost to herself.

"And you – you will stay in your room until I decide what to do with you," her father snapped.

"If that is what you wish. Congratulations on making an enemy out of your wealthiest neighbor," she said icily.

"Nonsense. His brother will understand I cannot permit this behavior."

"His brother will never understand anything again! Pemberley belongs to James now." She picked up the letter from the floor where it had fallen from her hand. Thrusting it at her father, she said, "Since you will not listen to *me*, you may read this. James came to me for comfort after losing what little family he still had, and you – you chased him away!" Tears in her eyes, she ran from the room before she said even more things she would regret.

In her room, she threw herself on the bed and sobbed, both for James's loss and her own. How could her father have refused to listen? Was this the man for whom she was sacrificing her own future happiness? James loved her, and now he needed her as well. If only she could go to Pemberley this minute! She would be able to comfort and support James at this terrible time. For a few moments she actually considered the idea of running off, but then she realized her father would already have set servants to watch her. There was nothing she could do.

It had been a brutal three days. James had attended the funerals for his brother and sister-in-law, as well as each of the four servants who had died as a result of the fire. The smell of smoke still permeated Pemberley. He had inspected the burnt-out rooms, noting the destruction of his father's bed and his mother's favorite vanity, the dark red velvet drapes he had loved to stroke as a child, and the painted shepherds on the walls. The portrait of his mother was unrecognizable, the paint charred and peeling. The staff was already hard at work clearing the rooms, but it would be months until they were fit for habitation. James was sleeping in the childhood bedroom he had shared with George, and the empty bed across from his haunted him.

He had met with the solicitors for the reading of his brother's will. It contained no surprises, but was surprisingly painful to listen to nonetheless, with its mentions of provisions for children yet unborn. Everything came to James, of course, since there was no one else. At the end, the solicitor had carefully removed his spectacles and reminded James of the urgent necessity of begetting an heir for Pemberley. Not that he intended to do anything about it; if he could not have Anne, he could not imagine marrying another woman. The few minutes he had spent with her before Lord Matlock threw him out had only confirmed what he already knew. She was the only woman for him.

Late in the day, he was astonished to discover Francis Fitzwilliam riding up on a lathered horse. Swinging out of the saddle, his friend said, "I came as quickly as I could. What can I do to help?"

James stared at him in bewilderment. "What are you doing here?"

"Anne wrote me and told me what had happened. We were worried in London, with no idea where you had disappeared to or why. No one thought you had deserted, but the Colonel sent out men to check the dead bodies found in the Thames. He was relieved when I told him about Anne's letter. She said you needed a friend."

Too exhausted by grief even to deny it, James just nodded. "It was good of her to inform you."

"She is frantic with worry and furious with our father, and says she would have run off if he had not set servants to watch her all the time. I *am* sorry, James."

James was not certain precisely whether Francis was expressing condolences about his brother or about Anne's unattainability, but it did not matter. He was glad to have a friend with him.

On the fifth day, Lady Anne approached her father. She had no expectation of a positive result, but she had nothing to lose. Her father could not possibly become any more set against James Darcy than he already was.

Lord Matlock barely looked up from his newspaper when she asked to speak to him. "What is it?" He sounded bored.

She clasped her hands together tightly. "The news from Pemberley was in the newspaper we received yesterday."

His eyes narrowed slightly. "It was."

"James Darcy has inherited everything."

"And nothing else has changed."

"You would have married me to his brother in an instant had the opportunity arisen. Why not James?"

"I cannot afford to have my debts called in, and I will not lose this estate. Besides, a broken betrothal would ruin you."

"If James does not care about a broken betrothal, why should you? Can you afford to turn down an alliance with Pemberley? It is one of the most profitable estates in Derbyshire, and the Darcys have no debt."

"Third most profitable, after Chatsworth and Calke Abbey. So you would have us lose everything, all the Fitzwilliam properties, even your mother's jewels, so you can marry your precious James?"

"James might be able to help you." She had hoped to avoid this, since she had no right to bargain with James's money. "He would not wish for you to lose this house."

"Oh, yes. No doubt I am the very first person who comes to his mind when he feels the urge to give away money," he said with a sardonic twist to his mouth. "I do not need his charity."

"No," she said evenly. "It is much simpler to sell your daughter than to take money from your neighbor."

He looked over the top of the newspaper at her. "Yes, it is. Especially when it means my daughter will live in luxury the rest of her life. A terrible fate indeed."

She was going to hate herself for this later. "Then give him Catherine. She wants to be rich, and she will never catch a rich man on her own."

"Too young. He has already waited six years, and will not wait two more."

"Then do not make him wait. I had to be well launched into society if I was to do him any good, but as Mrs. Darcy of Pemberley, I could launch Catherine even if they are already married. You could have both – your debts cancelled and a tie to the Pemberley coffers."

His expression did not change as he considered this for what seemed to be hours, but perhaps was no more than a minute. "No. This discussion is over." The newspaper rattled as he shook it out and raised it once again.

At least she had tried. Discouraged, she walked out to the stables and asked for her horse to be saddled. Naturally, two of the grooms had to ride behind her, but she did not object to that. It was part of her plan. She rode to the top of the tallest of the hills behind Matlock House, setting a pace on her thoroughbred that made it almost impossible for the grooms on their lesser horses to keep up.

Once atop the peak, she dismounted and sat on an exposed stone, her gaze turned towards Pemberley. It was too far away to see, and behind a ridge in any case, but she knew where it was. She wished she could somehow send the strength of her love to James. He would likely be in need of it.

The days at Pemberley blurred into a grey haze in James's mind. Francis had remained for a fortnight, assisting him with the grim duties of ordering mourning clothes, writing letters to friends and relatives, reading the condolences received, and deciding which of George's possessions were worth the effort to salvage. Now James had the harder task of stepping into George's shoes, a task for which he was sadly unprepared. He recalled now all the times his father had taken George with him on estate business, teaching him what he would need to know as Master of Pemberley, knowledge James now desperately needed.

He spent hours going through the estate books, trying to make sense of the accounting. The household was in chaos as well, since the housekeeper who had held the post as long as

James could remember had been a victim of the fire as well. At the steward's suggestion, James had appointed the housekeeper's assistant to the position. She was young for the task, and some of the staff seemed disinclined to listen to her at first, but they quickly saw she was efficient and hard-working for all her youth and inexperience. At least that was one problem solved.

Late at night, as he lay awake in his bed, he would think of Anne. Once matters were settled at Pemberley, he intended to call on her father. In his imagination, this meeting ranged from a mature discussion of the need for good relations between two nearby households to a furious denunciation of Lord Matlock's behavior towards him and a demand that he be allowed to marry Lady Anne. The only good thing to come out of all these changes was that as Master of Pemberley he could no longer be ignored as a potential suitor. He would prefer to have George back, but since that was impossible, he would reap what benefits he could of his new position. It would have to wait, though. Three months was the bare minimum he must remain in mourning for his brother. Even that was indecently short, but it would have to do. He ached for Anne.

One night as he was picking at his lonely dinner and missing the camaraderie of meals in the barracks, a footman told him a boy had arrived with a message for him, insisting on delivering it personally. James pushed his plate away with some relief as the messenger came in hesitantly.

"You have a message for me?"

"Are you Mr. Darcy? I can only give it to Mr. Darcy."

For a moment, James thought he must be referring to George, but then recalled *he* was now Mr. Darcy. Lieutenant Darcy was part of his past. "I am he." He held out his hand as the boy fished through a grubby pocket.

Instead of pulling out a letter, he presented a scrap of paper that had been folded over itself until it was small enough to hide in the palm of one hand. "Here it is, sir."

James frowned at the odd bit of paper. "Who gave you this?"

"A lady, a fine one. Don't know her name. She saw me when she was shopping in Matlock this morning, and she asked me if I wanted to earn some money. Said you'd pay me for it if I got it to you today," he said hopefully.

"And I shall," said James absently as he unfolded the scrap of paper. It held only a few words, printed in block capitals as if to disguise the handwriting. *The place you must climb – tomorrow.* He sucked in a deep breath. It had to be Anne. "What did this lady look like? Was she...was she short and plump?"

"Oh, no, sir. She was tall, as tall as a man."

A slow smile spread across James's face. His clever Anne, to use words only he would understand! Even if it had fallen into her father's hands, it would have meant nothing to him. But it meant the world to James.

He was there early the next day, earlier than she could possibly arrive, given that her father's estate was farther from the Black Rocks than Pemberley was, and she likely had more difficulty getting away than he did. He had no idea how she planned to manage it or whether she even would be able to come.

Nor was he certain where she expected to meet him. Was it atop the rocks, at the foot of the path, in the clearing below the path, or on the road? Finally he elected for the one place where she could not possibly miss his presence, and where he could see her coming. He tied his horse in the woods, then climbed the path until he reached the rocks.

The sun was well past its zenith when he spotted two ladies riding side-saddle. There had been several false alarms already, so he did not let his hopes rise until they turned onto the lane leading to the clearing. Then he scrambled off the rock tower and hurtled down the path, recklessly skidding down the steep sections until he neared the clearing. Hearing voices, he stopped just out of sight.

"I am so sorry, your ladyship, but I cannot go up there. I beg you, do not make me. I do not want to fall to my death!" It was a near-frantic female voice.

"Do not worry, Martha." Anne's familiar voice warmed him deep inside. "You may remain here, or even go back down to the road if you prefer. Nothing will happen to me if I go on my own. You can see there is no one else here."

"Your father will beat me!"

"My father will never know," said Anne briskly. "Wait here for me."

He heard the sound of gravel shifting under her feet as she came around the bend, the most beautiful sight he had ever seen. Then she ran into his arms, and he stopped thinking at all.

When they finally separated, albeit only by a few inches, she looked searchingly up at him. "You are thinner," she said. She touched the black armband on his sleeve. "It must be terribly difficult for you."

It was as if they had never been apart. "Sometimes it still does not seem real," he said, the words rushing out of him. "I expect George to run in at any moment, laughing at me for my credulous nature. I cannot accustom myself to giving orders at Pemberley. And I miss you – so, so much." He kissed her, trying to pour every bit of his love for her into it.

Her response was fervent. When she could breathe again, Anne said, "I cannot tell you how furious I was with my father that day! He was so horrible to you. I will never forgive him for that." She caught his hand. "But I want to go up to the top. Right now – and with you."

It was a slower trip than usual, owing to the need for frequent stops for kisses. The heavy weight that had been crushing James's chest for weeks was finally gone. Anne's light spirits lifted his as well. He would not think of how temporary this respite must be.

She sighed with happiness when they reached the summit, turning in a slow circle to take in the view. "It is just as glorious as I remember."

James pointed to the south. "Off in the distance you can see a lake with a line of trees leading up to it. That is Pemberley."

"I had not realized it was so nearby."

"Around ten miles." From behind her, he wrapped his arms around her waist and held her against his chest. How could anyone think her too tall? She was the perfect height. "How did you manage to get away? I thought your father would have you watched every minute."

"He did for a time. Then I started taking long rides every day, sometimes losing my escorts, but always coming back anyway. Eventually, they began to relax their guard, and now I can go out with only a maid. I was careful to bring one today who is terrified of heights so we could be alone."

"I hope there will not be trouble when you return. It will be very late by then."

She turned in his arms and, with a radiant smile, touched his cheeks with her hands. "I am not going back."

"What do you mean? Are you going somewhere else?"

"I am going wherever you go. I have been thinking hard these last few weeks, and I came to the conclusion you were right. I deserve the right to choose my own happiness rather than to pay off my father's sins. I saw him in a different light after that day when you came to see me, and if he loses everything he owns, it is no more than what he deserves. I will go to Gretna Green with you."

Relief flowed through him, accompanied by heartfelt joy. He experienced a moment of pure happiness, but then it struck him. There was a flaw in his pleasure. It should not matter why she was ready to elope with him now. He did not doubt she loved him, and if she believed she could not marry him when he had no fortune of his own, that was likely no more than good sense on her part. He would have been happy to marry her if she had been a pauper – and for all intents and purposes, she *was* a pauper now, or would be once her father disowned her. But he wished he could believe her choice was a disinterested one.

She looked at him with concern. "What is it? I thought you would be pleased." She hesitated, then added, "Do you no longer wish to marry me? Pray say so at once if that is the case, and I will trouble you no longer." Swallowing hard, she turned her gaze away from him.

"Anne, my dearest, do not say such a thing! Of course I wish to marry you. I have always wished for that."

"But you are not pleased. Do not lie to me; I can tell."

"I *am* pleased. I cannot quite take it in; I have been resigning myself to not having you for so long that it seems almost impossible. And..." He paused. It was true; she would know if he did not tell her the truth, and it would lie between them. "And I had not thought my lack of fortune played such a role in your choice not to marry me before. It does not matter; I understand you must be practical about these things. I just had not expected my inheritance to make such a difference to you."

"Your inheritance? Do not tell me you think the reason I changed my mind is because now you are rich! James Darcy, if there were not a hundred foot drop behind you, I would kick you!"

He held his empty palms out in a gesture of appeasement. "What else am I to think when you have refused me so many times in the past, yet as soon as I inherited Pemberley, you changed your mind?" If only she would argue with him!

To his dismay, her cheeks grew scarlet and she looked away. "I would have been happy to live in a cottage with you. It was not your fortune that changed my mind," she said quietly. "I wish that *were* my reason, because the true one is worse."

"Tell me, Anne. What are you keeping from me?"

She sighed heavily, then met his eyes. "Very well; I will tell you, but you must never, ever, *ever* tease me about it."

He took her hands. "I promise."

Pursing her lips, she looked upwards as if seeking inspiration. "In a way it *was* your inheritance that changed my mind, but not for the reason you think. In London, you told me you would never marry if you could not have me. I knew most likely you would change your mind some day, but it would be far in the future, so I did not worry about it. But that was before you inherited the estate. Now you would have to marry for Pemberley's sake. I could not stand it. The idea of you marrying another woman, of another woman bearing your children, made me ill. I could hardly force down a bite of food. And *that* is why I decided to disobey my father and leave my family – all because I could not bear the thought of you married to someone else. Do not laugh at me! I realize it makes me a hypocrite of the worst sort, because I had been willing to put *you* through that same misery." She still would not look at him.

Relieved beyond measure, he gathered her into his arms, pressing kisses against her forehead, her cheeks, and any other part of her he could reach. "My dearest love, that is nothing to be ashamed of, nothing at all. It means you love me. I hated the idea of you married to another man, but it was not the same thing. You had been promised to him long before I fell in love with you. You did not choose him over me."

He could feel the hitch in her breath as she pressed herself against his chest. "I truly would have been perfectly happy with a cottage," she said, her voice trembling.

"I know, my dearest. That was why I was so disturbed when I thought I had been mistaken."

"Then you will go to Gretna Green with me?" She sounded unusually tentative.

"I will go with you to Gretna Green, and I will most definitely marry you; on that you may depend. But it is just possible we may still be able to avoid the scandal of an elopement. I have an idea."

The following day James rode to Lord Matlock's estate. He and Anne had decided it would be better to wait a day rather than confronting him immediately. That way he would have more time to worry. Anne's father would have no means of knowing what had happened to her, since Anne's maid had wisely chosen to accompany her mistress to Pemberley rather than return to face Lord Matlock's wrath alone.

Apparently the tactic of leaving the Earl to worry had worked, since James was shown in to see him immediately. He strode in with all the confidence he could muster. After all, Anne would be his wife regardless of the outcome of this meeting, but he would prefer it if she could also maintain her ties to her family.

"What can I do for you, Darcy?" asked Lord Matlock calmly.

Expecting a tirade of abuse, James was somewhat taken aback by the Earl's lack of concern, but he rallied quickly. "My lord, by now I imagine you are aware that Lady Anne has run off."

"Someone may have mentioned it to me, if I recall correctly."

There was no doubt about it. Lord Matlock was toying with him. "Perhaps there is no point to my visit then, since you seem unconcerned about your daughter's whereabouts."

The Earl snorted. "Why should I have concerns about her whereabouts when I know perfectly well where she is? Your presence here is only confirmation of it."

"My presence here, my lord, is to offer you a choice. Lady Anne has gone to Scotland, and after I am done here, I will join her there. Whether we marry over the anvil in Gretna Green or return home is up to you. If you are prepared to give your consent to our marriage, we can have a proper church ceremony and spare you the scandal of an elopement in the family. It is your choice."

"You can marry her if you wish. It makes no difference to me."

James raised his eyebrows. "This is quite a change of tune from 'Throw him out and do not allow him to return.'"

Lord Matlock sighed. "Young man, if you are going to be running Pemberley, you had best learn a little strategic thinking. Do you really believe Anne would have been able to slip away if I had been set on preventing it? No, I am far better off if I can tell Berg with complete honesty Anne disgraced herself by running off against my express instructions, and that I had no choice but to patch things up and make the best of it. Then I can offer him Catherine in her place."

James merely looked at him for a long minute, then said coolly, "I am glad for Lady Anne's sake there is no need for Gretna Green because it might have troubled her conscience, but I have no intention of learning your *strategic thinking* if it involves lying to my future wife and causing her unnecessary pain as you have done. Neither my father nor my brother saw the need to manipulate their family to their own ends, and Pemberley seems to have thrived nonetheless – although I cannot say the same for Matlock. Good day, my lord." He turned on his heel to leave.

"You have some interesting illusions about your father," Lord Matlock said to his retreating back. "Some day I should tell you a few stories about him."

"I am sorry to have to inform you, my lord, that nothing you can say will in any way impede my happiness on this day of all days, so you might as well save your efforts for a more receptive audience."

Lord Matlock snorted.

Part III

Derbyshire, 1812

"So they did not marry at Gretna Green after all?" asked Elizabeth eagerly.

Darcy shot her an amused look. "Actually, they did, but told no one about it; and later had an official wedding in the church in Matlock They did not trust Lord Matlock to keep his word, so they chose to be prepared for all eventualities."

"So your father did manage a little strategic thinking of his own – and without lying!" Elizabeth felt oddly pleased by this.

"He did."

"Tell me, how did Lady Catherine avoid marrying the banker?"

"She did not avoid it. Mr. Berg was incensed over the substitution, and to placate him, Lord Matlock called in many favors in order to have him knighted. But Sir Lewis Berg was not good enough for him, so he changed his name to Sir Lewis de Bourgh. Were you to ask Lady Catherine, however, she will tell you he is from the ancient line of de Bourghs."

"I am learning a great deal today!" said Elizabeth.

"And here we are – the top of the outcropping is just ahead. But first..." He took a deep breath, apparently gathering resolve, then said, "As indelicate as this may be, if my mother were here, she would advise you to kneel once you are out on the rock. The wind can be brisk out in the open, and ladies' skirts easily turn into sails. It is not a place where you would wish to be caught off balance." His cheeks were flushed.

With a teasing smile, she said, "I appreciate your concern, Mr. Darcy, and you are no doubt wise to caution me. Tell me, did your mother kneel when she was on the rock?"

He looked down at the path beneath his feet. "When I was a child and would go out on the rock with her, she always knelt and kept an arm around me."

"*You* have been practicing strategic thinking, Mr. Darcy! Very well, I will take my answer from what you did *not* say – but I *will* be careful." Gathering her skirts, she scrambled up until she stood on the rock face. A few feet ahead of her, the rock protruded into open air, as if the hill had somehow stuck out a stony fist. This must be where she had seen Mr. Darcy standing earlier. Beyond this point, any misstep could send her plunging hundreds of feet to the ground. It was in equal parts terrifying and exhilarating. With an excited smile, she stepped out onto the rock over the abyss.

The view was nothing less than spectacular. Lines of hills ringed the broad valley beneath her, the fields delineated by dry stone fences like a patchwork quilt from this height. She could see shadows moving across the landscape as clouds scudded across the sky. This must be how the world wold look to a bird in flight! She stepped forward until she was practically at the end of the rock, elated by the sense of total freedom. Oh, if only she could remain up here forever! She let her eyes roam over the curves of the hills. How fortunate Mr. Darcy was to live so near this place!

Looking back over her shoulder to speak to him, she was startled to find him standing only inches behind her. His hand shot out to steady her, but he pulled it back when it became clear her footing was secure. "So," she said, oddly unnerved by his nearness, "In which direction does Pemberley lie?"

He pointed off to her left. "Between those two large hills. You can just see the sun reflecting off the water of the lake."

"Is that Pemberley House just beyond the lake?"

"Your eyes are sharp. I can barely make it out, but yes, that is the house." Standing directly behind her shoulder, he indicated several other points of interest around them.

Despite her interest in what he was telling her, her awareness focused on how close his body was to hers, his arm so near her own that the slightest movement would bring them into contact. It was a disconcerting sensation, almost as strange as standing hundreds of feet above the ground. She had never before noticed how mellifluous his deep voice was, with just a hint of gravel underneath the clear tone. Her arms prickled with goosebumps.

In her distraction, she had completely forgotten his warning about the wind, and so was unprepared when a strong gust came out of nowhere, sending her skirt and bonnet ribbons flying out like flags. She did not lose her balance – not quite, anyway – but she did stagger a little closer to the edge than was comfortable, making her heart pound so fiercely she could almost hear it.

Then a warm arm wrapped firmly around her waist, pulling her sharply back from the edge and up against a solid form. Good heavens – her back must be pressed tight against his chest! His quick breathing rushed past her ear. He must have been frightened as well, although she had been in no real danger of falling. No, it was a completely different sort of danger she faced, especially if her aunt or uncle happened to look up at the rocks just then. Darcy apparently shared her concerns, since he released her and took a step backwards.

Heat rose in her cheeks, and she hardly knew what to say. A distraction – that was what she needed. "When you were standing here earlier, I thought I saw you drop something over the edge. Was that my imagination?"

He did not answer immediately, and when he did, his voice was almost too even. "Rose petals, also in remembrance of my mother. She adored roses. My father had a special walled garden built so that she could grow them more easily, since the climate here is not overly hospitable to rose bushes. There were always little dishes of rose petals in every room, so the fragrance of roses was all around us. Bringing the rose petals here was my idea, but my father took part in it as well."

For some reason, the idea almost brought tears to her eyes. "It must have been very difficult for him when she died."

"He was never the same afterwards. He was always kind and attentive, but something was missing, some spark of warmth. I was not surprised when he took ill and died. It was almost as if he had only held on until I was old enough to care for my sister and for the estate. I grieved for him, but I knew it was what he had wanted – to be with her again." His voice was rough.

Impulsively she said, "Thank you for bringing me here, especially after you had just climbed it yourself. I would have hated to have missed this." She gestured at the panoramic view before her. "I could remain here all day."

"It has been my pleasure," he said formally. "But if you wish to stand so close to the edge, I would be happier if you permitted me to hold your wrist in case the wind picks up again. It is harder for me to watch you at the edge than it is to stand there myself."

She cocked her head at him. "I hope you are aware that I have never been knocked over by wind when I stood on solid ground, and there is no reason it should be different simply because I am standing on this particular rock."

His eyes flashed. "Sometimes reason has little to do with how we react when faced by such situations."

She had the odd feeling he was not speaking only of the risk of falling from the rock outcropping. How difficult this must be for him! He had spoken with such feeling about his father's affection for his mother. It was frightening to think that he might, like his father and grandfather before him, have that predisposition to attach himself to one woman, and one woman only. Of course, far from proposing quickly, he had fought his feelings for months and even tried to give her up, but she still did not know how deep his sentiments towards her ran. At that thought, a little voice inside her accused her of deceiving herself.

In this small matter, she could give him what he wished for. Holding out her arm to him, she said, "I do not wish to make you uncomfortable. I will even admit that, like your mother, if I were here with a child, I would likely choose the safer course of kneeling." It was a simple enough statement, so why did it make her light-headed, as if birds were taking flight in the pit of her stomach? She could stand over an abyss without fear of falling, but something about this man threw her off balance.

One side of his mouth quirked up as his hand closed around her wrist in a firm grip. "I thank you for your patience with me."

Elizabeth's mouth went dry. The determined pressure of his hand felt different than the light clasp of a dancing partner. Good heavens, what was the matter with her? She had longed to come to this place of astonishing beauty, and now she was there, all she could think about was Mr. Darcy's hand on hers. She was becoming as giddy as Lydia! "If I should slip now, sir, I shall pull you over the edge with me." She widened her eyes in mock innocence.

He muttered something to himself that she could not quite make out, apart from the words 'long ago.' She needed to pay less attention to him; that was all. But no sooner had she resolved to focus all her attention on her high perch and the invigorating panorama before her than she remembered Mr. Darcy's description of his parents kissing on this very rock.

Just then she felt pressure on her other wrist. Apparently he had decided to anchor her on both sides, even though it meant standing directly behind her. The hairs on the back of her neck prickled as she imagined how close he must be. She did not dare to look back at him, but unless he had contorted himself into some odd position, he must be close enough for it to take a deliberate effort to keep their bodies from touching. Her spine decided to turn into jelly at the thought.

Conversation. She needed to make conversation. "There are other rock outcroppings in the area, are there not? I recall seeing one when we passed through the town of Matlock."

"That is High Tor, near the Heights of Abraham. Did you visit the Savage Garden there?" His words were polite, but his tone was unexpectedly formal.

"Yes, although we could not stay as long as we would have wished, since it was growing dark. I enjoyed wandering the paths, even though I became lost once." Being lost had been far less disconcerting than her current circumstances, of which the least frightening aspect was standing a foot away from a sheer drop of several hundred feet. "I saw the rock formations in Dovedale as well. Such a lovely valley!"

She was glad to have tumbled upon the topic of her travels, since it allowed for a great deal of innocent conversation.

Her thoughts were less innocent, especially when she felt the warmth of his breath against her neck.

His answers grew briefer, and after a few minutes he said, "Miss Bennet, I believe we should return to your uncle and aunt now."

"Oh, must we?" she exclaimed. "It is so beautiful here."

"Yes," he said tersely. "We must."

Somehow she must have offended him, though she could think of nothing controversial in their conversation. So his new civility was only that; apparently his affections were more transient than his father's. "Of course. How thoughtless of me to keep you all this time when you were already on your way home!"

"It is of no importance." He sounded more like the haughty Mr. Darcy whom she had seen at the Meryton Assembly than the gentleman who had shared with her the intimate story of his parents' romance. But if he wished to leave, why had he not released her hands?

"Very well," she said, puzzled by the change in his demeanor. What was she to make of this man? He wanted to depart immediately for no apparent reason, yet continued to hold her wrists, making it impossible for her to turn back toward him. "I apologize for any inconvenience I have caused you." She hoped he would understand her apology was also meant to encompass the cruel things she had said at Hunsford

"It is no inconvenience, but I am only human." His voice was low and rough, and he spoke so close to her ear that she felt his warm breath. "All too human."

"I do not believe I have ever mistaken you for anything else. Certainly not a sheep or a wildcat, which would seem to be the only non-human creatures we might encounter here." Good heavens, she was babbling!

Still holding her wrists, he crossed them in front of her so his hands lay over hers, pulling her back toward him until she could feel his chest behind her. It was a shocking embrace, especially from strait-laced Mr. Darcy, but it was also shockingly pleasurable. The temptation to lean back into him was well-nigh irresistible. Something warm and soft grazed the side of her neck, and it was already over by the time she realized it was his lips.

"*That* is why I said we should leave, because otherwise temptation would get the better of me – but obviously it was already too late. I should not have brought you here." But his tone said otherwise.

"Because your father brought your mother here that day?" she asked, struggling to keep her voice from trembling. At least no one could question her choice not to push him away, given that it would likely involve stepping off the edge of the rock. Of course, what he was doing to her felt nearly as dangerous as plummeting to the floor of the valley – and she was astonished to discover she did not *want* him to stop.

His warm lips caressed her neck again. "Because you are too easy to confide in, your eyes too bright, your spirits too infectious, and every inch of you too tempting – and because you are wearing rosewater." The last phrase sounded almost pained.

Elizabeth laid her head back against his shoulder, uncertain whether she wished to offer him comfort or just to be closer to him. At least she assumed it was his shoulder. Whatever it was, it felt strong and safe, at least until his breath tickled her cheek. His lips followed, tracing a line of fire along her face. Instinctively, she turned her head into his kisses, until his mouth touched the very corner of hers. A wave of liquid heat shot straight through her.

The shocking sensation brought her back to herself, and made her remember where they were. She might not understand what was happening between them, but she knew it should not happen there. With a sharp indrawn breath, she firmed her resolve. "Perhaps, as you suggest, we should return to my aunt and uncle now." Her voice trembled.

"I have changed my mind," he murmured, his hands tightening over hers as he nibbled her earlobe.

Who knew that such delightful sensations could come from her ear? Firming her resolve, Elizabeth said, "Mr. Darcy, we are in plain view of anyone within miles of this place." Not to mention other climbers. She had not noticed any during their ascent, but she had been so wrapped up in Mr. Darcy's tale she might have failed to notice a regiment of Napoleon's soldiers marching past. And that was before he began to touch her!

He stiffened, then his hands released her. "My apologies, Miss Bennet." His voice was distant as he stepped back to clear her path. He made no effort to offer her his arm.

Elizabeth watched him from the corner of her eye as they began to walk. Once again, he offered her assistance on the steeper stretches, but this time he did not meet her eyes. Apparently he had taken her words as more of a rebuke than she had meant them to be, which was, she supposed, not entirely surprising, given that *she* was unsure what she had meant as well. He had every reason not to feel secure in having her good opinion. The story of his parents, and perhaps more importantly, the way he had told it to her, had caused a shift in her view of him; but he had no way of knowing that. The tense set of his shoulders and his averted gaze told her he was in pain.

The clouds had covered the sun, and she shivered in the cool breeze. Something had to be done. He had taken all the risks so far, and perhaps it was her turn now. Gathering her courage, she said, "Mr. Darcy, I have been wondering about that Darcy family tradition. Does it continue, or does it skip a generation from time to time?"

After a moment's hesitation, he said flatly, "The tradition continues."

She touched her tongue to her dry lips, her heart pounding. "Yet you said nothing to me for months after we became acquainted."

Almost reluctantly, he said, "True, but it does not necessarily follow that I did not *wish* to say anything during that time. Unlike my father and grandfather, I fought against the knowledge."

And that was the part that still stung. "Perhaps I was not the sort of woman you expected fate to throw in your path."

He still did not look at her. "No, and even without that, I did not want the tradition to be true. I wished to be perfectly rational in choosing a bride."

"I can easily believe *that* of you! Rationality seems to be one of your principles."

His brows drew together. "Not only that. It was not always comfortable to be the child of parents with such a strong bond, especially after my mother's death. It seemed...safer not to love someone with that intensity."

Especially if that someone happened to turn on him at the very moment of his proposal and abuse him in the strongest terms! With a sinking sensation, Elizabeth imagined for the first time how he must have felt that night...and since then as well, apparently. What had she, in her ignorance, done? She had treated him as if he had no genuine feelings, as if he were as hard as the rock they stood on, never once thinking about whether he might care about his parents or whether he could be hurt by her cavalier disregard for his declaration of love. Yes, he had been rude, but she had been cruel – and despite that his affections had not changed. Now she had hurt him once again, although this time the wound had been unintentionally inflicted.

His current withdrawal was so different from his earlier civility. She could not bear it. Nor could she bring herself to attempt to explain herself in the face of his distant expression. But she had to do something, even if it was improper. Seizing his hand before she could talk herself out of it, she led him down a side path past another rock outcropping. He followed without complaint, but his face was still drawn when she stopped just beyond the rocks, hopefully out of sight of anyone who walked past.

Obviously stronger measures were required. Fortunately, she had no objection to applying them.

Darcy had not been capable of rational thought since the moment he had spotted Elizabeth across the clearing. Even though she had not looked happy to see him, he could not resist the chance to spend even a few minutes in her company. Then, when he recognized her desire to climb the rocks – and how could he not have seen it, as attuned as he was to her expression and every breath she took – he had recognized the opportunity before him. If he offered to take her there, not only could he spend more time with her, but perhaps she might think a bit more kindly of him. But almost immediately his description of his father's proposal had offended her, and in a desperate attempt to gain her forgiveness, he had poured out the entire story of his parents' courtship, something he had never told anyone before. She had not seemed to mind, thank heavens, and had even appeared interested, her expression warmer than he could ever recall seeing when she looked at him.

Then he had ruined it all through his inability to resist the temptation she offered standing before him on the high tor – the feeling of inevitability, the hedonistic scent of roses, the taste of her skin under his lips. The wave of crushing despair when she told him to stop, and he realized the only reason she had tolerated so much was her other alternative would have involved stepping over the precipice, had almost sent him over the edge. He was left with only one goal: to avoid offending her any further. Not that it would do him any good, since she would never again allow herself to be alone with him. That moment of weakness had ruined any chance he might ever have with her.

And then came her incomprehensible question about whether the family tradition applied to him. Why had she asked, practically in as many words, whether he still loved her? It should have been obvious enough, but it was unlike Elizabeth Bennet to rub salt in an unhealed wound, and he had never, *never*, known her to ask such a personal and indiscreet question of anyone. He could not begin to comprehend it – or perhaps he *dared* not comprehend it.

When she took him by the hand and led him off the main path, he wondered what she planned to berate him for this time. Whatever it was, he would have to try to bear it with dignity. He was so busy attempting to brace himself that he almost did not register when she turned to face him, but he could not miss the astonishing moment when her arms slid around his waist and she leaned her head on his shoulder.

He froze, unable to believe it was real. Most likely dreaming or delirious, some rational part of his brain concluded, but his body told him he was definitely not asleep. If he was delirious, he only hoped to remain so for as long as possible.

If he offended her again now, he would never forgive himself. Striving for the utmost caution despite the temptation before him, he said, "Miss Bennet, I do not understand. I thought you wished me to stop." Despite his best intentions, his arms stole around her back. At least he managed to resist the urge to draw her closer to him and to take possession of her enticing lips.

She turned her face into his chest, perhaps to hide a blush, so all he could see was the top of her bonnet. Her voice muffled by his coat, she said, "I did not wish you to do it in plain sight of everyone within miles."

"But..." He paused. Could that possibly be all she had meant? He had been certain she was angry at him. But here she was, standing so close to him that he could almost feel the warmth of her. His body, on the other hand, seemed to be of the opinion she was much too far away. Apparently she agreed with his body, since she moved forward. His rational mind began to wave a white flag of surrender as his arms tightened convulsively around her.

Shifting his position, he urged her backwards until he could feel the cool, uneven pressure of stone on the back of his hands. "There. Now no one can see *you* at all, and I do not care who sees me. I do not care..." His voice dropped to a murmur. "...about anything at all – except you."

He had to see her face. With the utmost care, he slid his hands under her chin and captured her bonnet strings. Luck was with him; he managed somehow to untie the strings rather than knot them further, and he gently lifted off the bonnet to reveal the dark curls that had haunted his dreams for months. The scent of rosewater tickled his nostrils.

Elizabeth felt his unsteady breathing and the pounding of his heart, but was too embarrassed to look up. How could she meet his eyes after behaving in such a forward manner? Not that he seemed to object, and he had been even more forward earlier. Something tickled underneath her chin, then her bonnet strings fell to each side. Cool air brushed over her bared head as he lifted off her bonnet. Elizabeth felt as if she herself had been newly exposed, not just her hair – as if she had taken a desperate leap into shamelessness.

It was not merely the absence of her bonnet that affected her so strongly; after all, he had seen her without it more often than not. If she had removed it herself, it would have meant nothing. But *he* had removed it – and that was an intimacy deeper than she would have imagined. It left her utterly undone. Even the sensation of his body against hers, so overwhelming to her senses, was not as shocking as that.

Somehow she had never fully realized the breadth of his shoulders or the strength of him before, and had certainly never imagined he would carry the scent of musk and starched linen – and just a hint of dried rose petals.

The light caress of his fingers beneath her chin made her gasp, and she was unable to resist his gentle urging to raise her face. Even so, embarrassment made her keep her eyes on the intricate knot of his cravat and the firm chin above it.

"Elizabeth." His warm breath danced over her cheeks as he murmured her name, saying it slowly, as if it were a prayer or a holy incantation. His voice sent a rush of unfamiliar sensations through her, making parts of her feel turned inside out, as other parts seemed to take on a life of their own.

Finally she found the courage to raise her gaze. His face was closer to hers than she had realized, and his eyes were in shadow and impossible to read. "Yes?" she said breathlessly, as if she had been running a race, but all she had done was to lift her head.

His nostrils flared. "Unless you tell me you do not wish it," he said unevenly, "I am going to kiss you."

How could she think of anything beyond the anticipation making her tremble and her lips part? She struggled to regain her rationality, but something within her longed to succumb to his mesmerizing closeness. And what difference did it make? She had made her decision when she led him off the path. One little step was all it had taken, and everything else fell into place behind it – touches, kisses, and eventually marriage. Words were so much more complex than the currents of sensation created by his hand gently tracing down her spine.

All those thoughts came and went in an instant, and she had not made any protest. She saw Darcy's lips curving in a smile that spoke of heart-felt delight – and then she could no longer see anything because her eyelids closed of their own accord as Darcy's lips brushed hers in a tender caress.

Darcy had dreamed of this moment so often, but his imagination paled against the reality of kissing Elizabeth. There was sensual pleasure, of course, but he had not anticipated the need that flooded through him at the touch of her lips, the yearning for more of her, or the indescribable triumph he felt when she began tentatively to respond.

It should have been enough, more than enough, but he needed more. These last months of pain, recrimination, and emptiness had left a void within him only she could fill. What did propriety matter when Elizabeth was in his arms, her lips opening sweetly beneath his? His hands had already discovered her dress was fastened with only four buttons and memorized the location of each for future reference, seemingly having decided of their own accord that anything happening in the narrow space between her back and the rock outcropping was fair game. And that tempting flesh above the dress! Silky smooth, and she shivered as his fingers drifted along her neckline. Intoxicated by the headiness of Elizabeth's response, he allowed his fingertips to dip just a fraction of an inch below her neckline, taking possession of the hidden flesh there.

Elizabeth gasped and arched herself against him, and that was his undoing. Until then, he had maintained some modicum of control, but now even that was slipping. After all, no one was likely to discover them there, and his desperate desire to taste every bit of Elizabeth's sweetness was on the verge of overwhelming his awareness of where they were and how utterly improper this was. He should stop, but that would give her time to become angry over his behavior, and then he would never again hold her in his arms, aching with the need to make her his. What had happened to the man who had been shocked by the knowledge that his father had kissed his mother on top of the Black Rocks in full view of the rest of the world?

But he could feel tension rising in her body and a new resistance to his embrace. Somehow he found the strength to wrench himself away from her. Struggling for control of his unruly body, he said hoarsely, "There are disadvantages to being out of sight as well. You would be unwise to trust me too much."

Elizabeth, still lost in the passionate haze he had created in her, could only stare at him. He was right, of course, but his kisses had been so pleasurable, and now she felt oddly cold and incomplete without his body pressed against hers. "I see," she said shakily.

He rubbed his hand over his jaw, then turned away from her, his lips tight and his hands clenched into fists. Why should he be troubled? He had wanted to kiss her, even if she had been the first to touch him this time. Perhaps he did not approve of her forward behavior, even if he enjoyed the results. In many ways she still hardly knew him, after all. There were bound to be surprises.

She bent down to recover her bonnet, then slowly set it on her head. Her fingers felt oddly clumsy as she tied the ribbon beneath her chin. Mr. Darcy still looked out into empty space, his back to her.

Taking a deep breath, she said, "Perhaps we should start down before those dark clouds come this way. I would not like to attempt the path when it is wet."

For a moment she thought he might not answer, then he said in a low voice, "I want you to tell me when you do not wish me to do something."

"I beg your pardon?"

He turned to face her, his expression hard. "I allowed matters to go too far. You must tell me when you are uncomfortable. I do not wish to make you unhappy."

"You did not make me unhappy. Nothing you did...," she said, her cheeks growing hot with the admission. "It was just rather sudden."

"That is all? Are you certain?"

The corners of her lips turned up. "Quite certain."

Darcy opened his mouth as if to say something, hesitated, and instead pulled her into his arms again. This time, though, he did not try to kiss her. Instead he cradled her to him as if she were a precious treasure.

Elizabeth's head rested on his shoulder. How was it that a mere embrace could bring her such happiness and pleasure? Or was it only when embracing the correct person? "Perhaps there is something to be said for your family tradition after all."

He pressed a kiss on her forehead, then released her reluctantly and offered her his arm instead. "I cannot deny it, even if I was foolish enough to fight it for so long. I was enchanted by you before we had exchanged half a dozen sentences."

"I am certain most of *my* sentences were impertinent!"

"Some of them were, but it does not follow that I did not enjoy hearing them. I was not as successful at resisting the tradition as it might have appeared. I almost made you an offer on the night of the Netherfield Ball."

For some reason, that surprised her. "As early as that?"

A slow smile crept over his face. "My father would have asked why I moved so slowly."

"It is just as well you did. I have enough reason to blush for my behavior toward you that night without adding the scene that might have been provoked, had you declared your intentions!"

His expression sobered. "After our dance, even I could sense you were in no mood to receive my assurances."

"I am sorry," she said impulsively.

"It was just as well nothing occurred that night. I was conscious of the hypocrisy of telling Bingley that he could not possibly be certain of his feelings for your sister after knowing her but six weeks when I was quite certain of my feelings for you."

Mr. Bingley! She had completely forgotten him, even though Jane still suffered from the loss of him. Her new connection with Mr. Darcy would put Jane in a difficult position. She would have to speak to him further about that, but not now. This time was too precious.

They had once again reached the narrow part of the path, bringing conversation to a halt. Elizabeth was just as glad of it; her thoughts were in such a whirl she doubted her ability to make sensible conversation. Two days ago she had no wish to ever see him again, and she had assumed he would feel the same way about her. And now... had she truly let him kiss her? What had she been thinking? And now she wanted so badly for him to do it again!

Traversing the steep path in her half-boots required her to watch her step, so she almost bumped into Mr. Darcy when he stopped in front of her. Startled, she looked up at him, immediately lost in the intensity of his dark eyes. Something about his look made her forget to breathe.

"Elizabeth," he said softly, "once we turn this corner, we will be in sight of your uncle and aunt."

"Oh." How foolish she must sound, but she could think of nothing else to say. He could not kiss her here, even if he wished to; although her aunt and uncle would not see, anyone ascending the path could do so easily.

With deliberation, he took her hand and raised it to his lips, pressing a slow kiss on her fingers. Finally he lifted his lips and turned over her hand. When he repeated the gesture on the inside of her wrist, she felt awareness spark deep within her, making her breathing ragged.

His chest was moving unevenly as well, and his eyes had grown even darker. "Come," he said, his voice rough. "Your aunt and uncle will be wondering what has happened to us."

Elizabeth was tempted to say they would not be the only ones wondering that, but swallowed the words. Their understanding was still too fragile to risk with that sort of teasing.

As he had predicted, the clearing came into view, with the Gardiners on the far side. This final descent was one of the steepest, and Darcy turned more than once to offer her a supportive hand. He would have looked the perfect gentleman from across the clearing, but the fire in his gaze indicated something quite different.

To Elizabeth's chagrin, she discovered the Gardiners watching them unusually closely. Good heavens! What was she to tell her aunt and uncle? Just the previous day she had claimed a passing acquaintance with Darcy, and now – well, she was not sure what she would say now. He had not actually proposed to her this time, though he seemed to assume they had an understanding. Either way, there would be questions to answer; that much was certain.

"I hope the climb was not too strenuous for you, Lizzy. You look a little flushed," said Mrs. Gardiner pointedly as the pair reached them.

Darcy had to force himself to look away from Elizabeth, who was now rather more flushed than she had been before.

Elizabeth said, "I suspect our jaunt took more of a toll on Mr. Darcy. I believe I tried his patience at times."

"Or something," he murmured just loud enough for her to hear. To the others he said, "Miss Bennet was more than patient as she listened with every impression of enjoyment to dull stories of people she has never met."

She looked up at him through her lashes. "I found your stories quite illuminating."

"I hope we have not delayed you overlong," said Darcy. "If you are able to spare the time, I hope to persuade you to visit Pemberley during your stay in Lambton. I would be happy to show you the house and grounds; and Mr. Gardiner, if you are fond of fishing, we have a particularly fine trout stream in the park. I can supply you with fishing tackle and show you the best spots."

"That is very kind of you, Mr. Darcy. I am indeed fond of fishing."

"Excellent. Might I impose on you, Mr. Gardiner, to walk with me for a few minutes?"

Mr. Gardiner exchanged a glance with his wife. "It would be my pleasure."

"I thank you." Darcy did not dare to look at Elizabeth as he escorted her uncle out of earshot of the ladies. "Mr. Gardiner, I imagine you are wondering why I requested this conference."

"I confess to some curiosity, though I daresay it involves my niece."

He took a deep breath. "It does. You were good enough to entrust Miss Bennet to my care earlier. I am sorry to report I did not live up to your trust. I am not proud of this, but I must tell you that I kissed your niece. I am not aware of anyone who was in a position to observe it, but I cannot be certain no one saw it."

Mr. Gardiner folded his hands behind his back, his expression serious. "I wonder why you are choosing to tell me this."

Admitting he hoped Mr. Gardiner would insist on his niece marrying him seemed a poor plan. "My self-control may have been lacking, but there is nothing amiss with my sense of responsibility."

"And what does my niece say of this?"

What a damnable question! "I did not ask her. The last time she and I discussed the matter did not end well owing to...some mutual misunderstandings, so I thought it better to seek permission to address her this time."

"Lizzy refused you? How interesting. Yet today she went off with you happily enough," Mr. Gardiner said thoughtfully.

Did the man not understand he was supposed to pin Darcy to a tree and demand he marry Elizabeth? "Some of the misunderstandings have been laid to rest."

"Well, Mr. Darcy, the question I must ask is whether you kissed Lizzy against her will."

At last, solid ground to stand on. "Ah...no, it was not against her will."

"I am glad to hear it," said Mr. Gardiner mildly, "since otherwise my next question would be whether you are very brave or merely foolhardy. I am not blind, nor is my wife, and we could see that rock outcropping clearly enough to tell you were standing remarkably close to Lizzy. We hoped it was not the prelude to watching Lizzy push you over the edge."

A reluctant smile tugged at Darcy's lips. "I imagine Miss Bennet would not hesitate to defend herself if she felt the situation warranted it."

"No, indeed. So, is it my permission to address her that you are seeking? I cannot speak for her father, naturally."

"Of course not, but as she is in your care at the moment, it is only fitting that I speak to *you*."

"It seems to *me* you should be addressing your question to Lizzy, not to me – but for some reason you seem remarkably hesitant to do so. I wonder why that might be."

Darcy scowled. Why did this particular one of Elizabeth's relations have to prove insightful, rather than a fool like all the rest? He did not wish to tell him Elizabeth's words at Hunsford still echoed in his head, and despite all the evidence she had given him in the last half hour, he feared another disaster. He had almost blurted out a proposal after their kiss, but the memory of the last time had frozen the words in his mouth.

Impulsively, he decided the truth was his only option. "Because the last time I made her an offer, I said something with the intention of pleasing her, but instead it offended her for reasons I could not comprehend, and she flew into a temper and refused to allow me to explain myself. Should that happen again, I want you to make her stay long enough to listen to what I have to say."

Mr. Gardiner regarded him quizzically for a moment and began first to chuckle, then to guffaw. When he finally regained his composure, wiping the corners of his eyes to remove tears of mirth, he said, "Indeed, I think Lizzy really ought to marry you, and I will tell her so."

Forcing himself to swallow his ire at the other gentleman's laughter, Darcy said tersely, "I thank you."

"No need to get up on your dignity, lad; I was not laughing at *you*. Apparently you are unaware Lizzy does not take offense or lose her temper easily, nor have I ever known her to refuse to listen to someone. When a woman behaves that uncharacteristically with a gentleman and then allows him to kiss her, you may rest assured her feelings are far from indifferent."

"So if she *had* pushed me over the edge of the cliff, that would have been a sign she *really* liked me?"

"Oh, yes," said Mr. Gardiner. "Otherwise she would simply talk circles around you, and you would never realize quite how she had managed to tie you in knots. That is what she usually does. But I already knew she was not indifferent to you."

"You did?" Darcy could not hide his astonishment.

"I remember telling my wife so at Christmas. Lizzy had taken such a pointed dislike to you I knew it had to mean something, and normally she would have better sense than to listen to that fellow who was always finding fault with you, the one who made love to everyone and smiled except when he thought no one was looking."

"George Wickham." Darcy ground out the name between his teeth.

"That is the one! But there is no need to fret, lad; he is long gone and *you* are the one who is kissing her on the sly."

Perhaps Mr. Gardiner had a point there. He was obviously a man of good sense if he had spotted that Wickham was not to be trusted. "Have you any advice for how I might best approach Miss Bennet on the subject?"

Mr. Gardiner clapped him on the shoulder. "Leave it to me, lad; leave it to me."

Darcy was quite happy to take that advice.

Mr. Gardiner was as good as his word. As soon as they returned to the spot where Elizabeth and Mrs. Gardiner were packing up their picnic, he said, "Well, Lizzy, Mr. Darcy has been explaining to me why he believes it would be a good idea for you to marry him."

She glanced up at her uncle with an amused look. "I see," she said, her voice neutral.

"I believe he would be interested in your opinion on the matter. Under the circumstances, I must say I am as well."

"My opinion?" She arched an eyebrow. "I had not realized it was of any great importance."

"Not of great importance?" her uncle spluttered.

She tilted her head as if considering the matter. "When a gentleman spends quite some time telling me in detail about his father's courtship of his mother, I have to assume there is some moral for me in the tale. Since in this case that courtship consisted primarily of his father insisting repeatedly they were to marry and his mother refusing him almost as often, I take the moral to be that there is very little point in refusing, since it would only lead to the question being repeated until I agreed to it out of sheer exhaustion. He would, however, likely be more comfortable to discover *some* resistance from my family, so perhaps *you* should refuse to allow him near me, or at least refer to him now and then as a worthless cur."

Mr. Gardiner chuckled. "I am sorry to disappoint you, my dear, but I am afraid that is out of the question. It might interfere with my fishing plans. You will have to quarrel with Mr. Darcy on your own."

At last she looked up at Darcy, her fine eyes sparkling. "Now that is a task I can definitely manage. We have a veritable talent for quarreling, do we not, Mr. Darcy?"

"At the moment, Miss Bennet, I am only inclined to quarrel about whether your recent response to the question of marriage constitutes an affirmative or a negative."

She eyed him with mock calculation. "Well, that depends."

It must be a good sign that she was teasing him, even if it was also driving him out of his mind. "And on what does it depend?"

"Should I agree, how often would you be willing to bring me here to climb the rocks?"

His face relaxed into a smile. "As often as you wish, my dear."

"Then I suppose I shall have to agree. Had you told me months ago Pemberley had such fine rocks for climbing, we might have settled matters between ourselves much sooner; but instead, everyone seemed set on informing me about foolish things like its beautiful façade, furnishings and grounds. I cannot think why anyone would find *those* things of such appeal."

"So you are marrying me only for the Black Rocks?"

"I did not say that. The walled rose garden helps as well.

"I see. My mother would approve."

A warm smile bloomed on her face. "I do hope so. I would hate to disappoint her."

Now that Elizabeth had stopped teasing, the welcome and happiness in her voice could not be mistaken. Darcy felt as dizzy as if he stood with one foot off the edge of the Black Rocks. Could this be true? Elizabeth had accepted him and looked pleased about it! His heart was so full he could think of nothing to say or do – at least nothing he could do in front of her aunt and uncle.

Mr. Gardiner cleared his throat. "Lizzy, it would be a kindness on your part to spare Mr. Darcy the embarrassment of asking my permission for a few minutes alone with you."

Darcy decided Mr. Gardiner was a gentleman of *eminent* good sense.

As they strolled away from the Gardiners, Elizabeth said, "You look stunned. I hope it does not mean you disapprove of my uncle."

"Far from it! So much has happened that I have reason enough to be amazed without him. I still can hardly believe you are really here this time, much less looking on me with favor."

Elizabeth cocked her head. "*This* time? Was there another time?"

"When I first saw you across the clearing, I told myself I must be mistaken. So many times in these last few months I have thought I spotted you – passing on the street, across the theatre, at the other end of a ballroom. But it always turned out to be another woman with hair like yours, whose movements were light and pleasing like yours, or who wore a dress similar to one I had seen you wear. So today I assumed I was mistaken once again, hoping to spare myself disappointment, but then you looked up at me and I knew it *was* you. I still cannot fully credit it, much less that you have accepted me."

An odd feeling coiled in the pit of Elizabeth's stomach. How little she deserved such devotion as his – and how grateful she was to have it! "You may believe it this time," she said softly.

"You may have to remind me of that frequently. It is too easy to believe you think ill of me – or that I frightened you with my kisses."

She looked up at him through her lashes. "I, frightened? When only a few feet away there was a perfectly good cliff I could push you over?"

He laughed, a joyous, free sound. "My mother would have liked you."

"For threatening to murder her son? How singular of her!" With a sidelong glance, she said, "I was *not* frightened, although *you* appeared somewhat out of sorts after...after you kissed me."

He gave a low laugh. "Out of sorts? You might as well say I was angry; and it would be true. Angry I could not trust my self-control any further, angry I had to stop when every instinct told me not to, angry I had already made demands of you that could easily have frightened you away. But angry with *you*? Not a bit." He raised a finger to stroke her cheek. "Believe me, what I wanted to do with you had nothing at all to do with anger."

"Goodness!" Elizabeth could feel the flush rising in her cheeks. "Perhaps it is just as well I did not know *that*."

His finger moved to trace her lips. "Have I shocked you?" He sounded distinctly pleased by the idea.

"*Surprised* me, perhaps. What has happened to the sober Mr. Darcy I thought I knew?"

"You cannot expect sobriety, my dearest Elizabeth, when you have just given me my heart's desire! As it is, I am showing remarkable restraint."

"If this is restraint, I hesitate to think what the alternative might be!"

"I could list a great number of alternatives for you, and I would doubtless enjoy telling you some of them, although not as much as I would enjoy putting them into action." He leaned down until his breath tickled her ear. "Here is a relatively tame one for you. Having kissed you atop the Black Rocks, according to my family tradition, I should now be entitled to take you back to Pemberley with me and thence to Gretna Green. Now tell me – am I not showing great restraint by allowing you to leave with your aunt and uncle?"

She could not help laughing at this unexpected side of Mr. Darcy – her future husband! "Great restraint indeed, sir! I am suitably impressed."

His eyes darkened. "Tread carefully, my love – you do not know how tempted I am to kiss you right now, despite your uncle watching us."

With an arch smile, she teased, "What a pity I did not think to leave my reticule or my gloves atop the rocks! Then we would have an excuse to walk up again. But *you* have already climbed the rocks twice today, so I doubt that idea has any appeal for you."

"Elizabeth," he said in a low voice. "You are playing with fire. I am now practicing the *most extreme* restraint."

Elizabeth had felt safe standing on the rock, but now, in response to his heated gaze, she feared her legs might give way under her. "I am duly warned! Instead of wishing to climb the rocks with you again, I will reflect on my good fortune in encountering you here at all. Otherwise I could not have climbed them even once – and I likely would never have seen you again." The idea was oddly frightening. How shockingly her sentiments towards him had changed in the last hour! The Darcy men might be the fastest at falling in love, but she defied anyone to challenge her for rapidity of changing her mind about a man.

He shook his head. "We would have met again in any case. I already spoke to Bingley about returning to Netherfield in the autumn. My avowed reason was to see whether your sister was still partial to Bingley, and if she were, to make a certain confession to him. My *real* purpose was to see *you*, and to judge whether I might ever hope to make you love me." His face was lit by a sudden smile. "The Darcy family tradition cannot be ignored, after all."

"Of course it cannot!" It made her heart swell to know he had not completely given up on her despite her harsh words at Hunsford – and that he wished to bring Jane and Bingley back together. "But it is better we met here. The rocks could not have worked their particular magic on me in Hertfordshire."

"Magic? I prefer to think of it as my mother and father watching over me," he said austerely. "But mostly I prefer to think of *you*."

Mrs. Gardiner looked after the retreating pair. "Good heavens," she said to her husband. "This is certainly not what I expected of the day. It was exciting enough to meet the famed Mr. Darcy of Pemberley. Am I now to understand that Lizzy, after an accidental meeting, has accepted an offer of *marriage* from him?"

"Apparently so," said her husband, his eyes twinkling. "It seems there is more to this story than our Lizzy has chosen to tell us. That young man appears to be quite violently in love with her, and if I am not mistaken, she has been leading him on a merry chase! Did she say anything to you while I was talking to him?"

"I asked her what had passed between them while they stood on the rock, and she gave me a long, mumbled explanation to the effect that Mr. Darcy insisted on holding her hand, as he was afraid she might fall because his father's twin brother was afraid of heights and died in a fire that was somehow related to rose petals and a cottage. Or at least those were the bits that I was able to comprehend." She shook her head in disbelief. "It was *most* unlike her. What did he say to you?"

Mr. Gardiner laughed. "As near as I can tell, he was trying very hard to convince me I ought to hold a pistol to his head and demand that he marry Lizzy, and he was singularly unconvincing. I was afraid the poor lad might have an apoplexy when I kept ignoring his hints!"

"Well, this trip is certainly proving to be a memorable one! They do make a handsome couple, I must say." She paused and sniffed the air. "How odd. I could have sworn I just smelled roses."

Her husband looked around them, his brow furrowed. "I thought I caught a whiff of them as well. Perhaps it is a wildflower with a similar scent." He reached over and took his wife's hand.

Across the clearing, Mr. Darcy leaned close to Elizabeth, whispering something that made her laugh. The sun chose that moment to break out from behind the clouds, bathing the couple in the full warmth of its rays.

Acknowledgements

Many people assisted in the creation of this novella. I'd like to thank Maria Grace, Cassandra Grafton, Susan Mason-Milks, and Elaine Sieff for their feedback on the manuscript. It is a better story thanks to them. My fellow Austen Authors (www.austenauthors.net) provided support, knowledge, and general encouragement. As always, conversation with my readers helped shape the work in progress. I'm grateful to live in an age where I can connect so easily to readers and other writers.

About the Author

Abigail Reynolds is a great believer in taking detours. Originally from upstate New York, she studied Russian and theater at Bryn Mawr College and marine biology at the Marine Biological Laboratory in Woods Hole. After a stint in performing arts administration, she decided to attend medical school, and took up writing as a hobby during her years as a physician in private practice.

A life-long lover of Jane Austen's novels, Abigail began writing variations on *Pride & Prejudice* in 2001, then expanded her repertoire to include a series of novels set on her beloved Cape Cod. Her most recent releases are *Mr. Darcy's Noble Connections*, *Mr. Darcy's Refuge*, *A Pemberley Medley*, and *Morning Light*, and she is currently working on a new Pemberley Variation and the next novel in her Cape Cod series. A lifetime member of JASNA and a founder of the popular Austen Variations group blog, she lives on Cape Cod with her husband, two children, and a menagerie of animals. Her hobbies do not include sleeping or cleaning her house.

www.pemberleyvariations.com
www.austenvariations.com

Join Abigail on
Facebook at www.facebook.com/abigail.reynolds1
Twitter @abigailreynolds

Also by Abigail Reynolds

The Pemberley Variations

What Would Mr. Darcy Do?

To Conquer Mr. Darcy

By Force of Instinct

Mr. Darcy's Undoing

Mr. Fitzwilliam Darcy: The Last Man in the World

Mr. Darcy's Obsession

A Pemberley Medley

Mr. Darcy's Letter

Mr. Darcy's Refuge

Mr. Darcy's Noble Connections

The Darcys of Derbyshire

The Woods Hole Quartet

The Man Who Loved Pride & Prejudice

Morning Light

 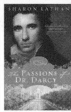   
   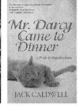 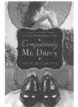
  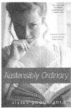  

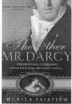

Made in the USA
Lexington, KY
30 June 2014